Hallowed HORRORS

HALLOWED HORRORS

This book is for entertainment purposes only.

Library of Congress Control Number: 2024937695

Printed in United States of America

ISBN: 979-8-9880338-7-5

Table of Contents

SUNDEBRENNEN

BERT LESTRANGE

Earthy tones of pine and spiced apple swirled over the decay of crackly brown leaves. Luscious amber, pale green, and radiant reds feathered branches that would all too soon be barren. Autumn was made for adventure, but October, specifically, was meant for remembrance. It's the time of year to think back on choices, reap final harvests, and remember the fallen. One last chance for atonement before nature spirits rest and winter's bitter chill steals life and light from the world.

Hannah and David arrived in Maistadt just as twilight's pale umbra descended. A thirty-mile drive through twisting forest roads took more than an hour, even with GPS for guidance. The city was hardly marked on any map, entirely absent from internet forums and travel guides. But the neighboring towns had spoken of the coming harvest festival with such reverence and excitement, it was impossible for digital nomads to ignore.

Unique content was becoming ever more difficult to come by. This opportunity was butter-basted, bacon-wrapped gold.

Through the forest twists afternoon light bent in obscure ways and the last few miles proved to be the worst of it. As the sun descended, filling the horizon with golden orange and bruisy purple, miles and miles of corn inked long shadowy tendrils as though reaching for them. Especially disconcerting due to both the vast expanse covered in swaying stalks and the unsettling frequency of scarecrows. Shiny black eyes watched them pass with all the callous indifference of a three-day corpse. They were clearly shirking their duties as crows stood four and five wide along each stick shoulder.

For all the familiarities, they felt as transient explorers in an enigmatic land. This strange country seemed to draw them back to a previous century and the village did nothing to dissuade this notion. Fachwerkabu style architecture lent a distinctly German, medieval quality.

A low wall of stacked stone encircled the town, its entrance too small for their car to pass. Cobblestones pimpled the streets, worn smooth with centuries of use and rather than modern electrical lights, proper flames flickered ominously in ancient brass coal gas lamps at the corner of every street. The last of these bloomed to life as they strolled, hand in hand, inside the city. A snow-haired, bearded fellow lowered his lighting pole with a grin. He sported a brown top hat and large-buttoned, brown uniform with a crimson half-cloak over his shoulders.

His accent was so thick that the couple initially thought he was speaking his native tongue rather than English.

Soon enough, he chauffeured them to a building whose wordless sign boasted two overflowing mugs and a bed.

The patrons within drank, sang, and feasted on baked pretzels, brown ale, and a variety of sausages with stone-ground mustard.

A beautiful woman in her early twenties spotted the couple, immediately locking ice-eyes with David, much to Hannah's annoyance. She tossed long, golden braids, beaming and arching her back ever slightly to accentuate the low cut of an otherwise traditional dirndl. Hannah pinched David's arm as the girl turned back to the bar, but not before bending over unnecessarily to reveal a noticeable lack of undergarments.

David's apologetic eyes met Hannah's raised eyebrow. "She's cute.

Good thing she can't get pregnant from being eye-fucked, huh?"

"I... Uh, she caught me off guard. It was a long drive... Sorry, I'm an idiot sometimes."

Hannah smirked. "At times, but you're a good boy sometimes too. Keep your eyes to yourself, arms and legs inside the ride at all times, and I'll remind you of what you have later."

"Yes ma'am!" He looked relieved.

When the waitress returned, David looked everywhere except at her, even when she came inches from his nose to drop off two pewter steins of unordered beer.

"Americans, if I'm nicht mistaken. Are you here fur ze festifal?" Her voice was bright and sparkled like her eyes.

Long, curly lashes batted as she bit her lower lip.

David suddenly found one of the hewn ceiling beams particularly interesting. Hannah took note with more than a little pride.

"For that and only that, yes. Freshly arrived. Is there somewhere in town where we can rent rooms?" Hannah asked with an aggressive tone that surprised even her.

The girl beamed and dimples perked in her cheeks. Her teeth were perfect, whiter than paper. "Oh good. Vonderful! Ja, ve haf rooms. Two only or vil you haf guests also?"

"Two? No, we'll only need one room. We're together. Engaged actually." Hannah flashed her ring. "No guests, just one room. It's just us."

The girl's forehead wrinkled, then she shook her head. "No."

"No?" Hannah frowned. "What do you mean 'no'?" She asked.

Even David chanced an incredulous look.

"It's nicht done zat vay. Men undt vomen. Zey to nicht mix togezzer." She pointed to the dual staircases on either side of the bar in turn. "Menfolk. Vomenfolk. Zere are laws, sorry!"

The girl bounced on her toes, noticing David's gaze one more directed at her. "I'm Helga and I vill hentle your needs."

"Maybe we should sleep in the car?" David asked.

Hannah made a face. "The festival is three days out. I'm not sleeping in the car for three days. It'll be fine. Two rooms."

"Zen velcome to Maistadt! Enchoy ze show!"

David collected their luggage while Hannah held down the table. Between the beer and bread, the couple soon found themselves nearing carbohydrate comas. As the tavern had mostly cleared. Even the flirty waitress had gone home for the night.

Hannah yawned, wrapping her arms around his neck. "I had every intention of fucking your brains out tonight. I swear."

"Raincheck. It's going to be a long, lonely night." He put his lips against her forehead, drawing her close.

They shared another quick kiss and ascended the respective stairs. Each blew the other a kiss from across the upstairs banisters.

The rooms were simple, but comfortable. Including only a plush feather bed and an ornately carved writing desk with matching chair. A rolled-up bathrobe looked like a swan. One simple window looked out to the nearby, snowy mountains. As it turned out, the bathroom was down the hall, a communal affair, which explained the segregation of sexes.

Hannah crawled under the cloud-like covers and passed out in moments.

Having driven more than ten hours that day, David was stiff and sore. If he slept now, he'd wake up a miserable tangle of cricks and creaks. A hot shower would make all the difference.

He unpacked and undressed, donning the robe before trudging down the hall. Similar to the bed, the robe was soft, warm, and fluffy. Combined with the carb-drowsiness, he felt like a cozy little pancake.

Pleasantly surprised, David found the blue epoxy and river stone floors to be heated against his bare feet. The decor was intended to mimic an oceanside basalt cave. And beyond the tasteful doors, light fixtures, and sinks, it did a fairly good job.

A perfect circle of stacked black stones with a glass door made to match revealed the shower. It was huge. Ten men or more could share the space at once without touching shoulders, even with extended arms. David turned on each one in turn and soon steam drifted from the floor to his shoulders.

Little refillable containers of shampoo, conditioner, and body wash were attached to the wall beneath each shower head.

David spent the first twenty minutes letting the warmth soak deep into his bones. The moist heat against his eyelids was so satisfying. He'd been running on caffeine and adrenaline for most of the past week.

Their funding was steadily drying up without enough coming in to replace it. At this rate, they had less than two months before they were totally broke. When he brought it up Hannah exploded, and they hadn't spoken for a couple of days. It was hell to share a car with someone who wanted to be anywhere else. That had been three weeks ago.

Tonight, had been the first time she'd seriously mentioned intimacy since the "event". There had been a few other times, but those proved empty, unintentionally cruel promises. That frustration steeped into a bitterness he couldn't wash out.

Helga's dimpled smile flashed in his mind. Perfect mouth, eyes like sapphires, dangerous curves, and no inhibitions about letting someone know she was interested. His hand slipped down into the mist, and he groaned with pent up desire. Her pigtails like handlebars, thick accent screaming his name... the fantasy was intoxicating. He couldn't believe how wound up he was, especially being so tired.

He was so caught up in it, in fact, that he didn't feel a momentary chill sweep through the steam.

It wasn't until she pressed her bare ass against his hips that he noticed someone had joined him. He drew back, but she had hold of his thighs and pulled herself against him once more. Fumbling through the mist, he found long, blonde pigtails. Each night afterward, she would come to his room, and each night she provided the release he so desperately craved.

He moaned and gave in, unable to control himself any longer.

***

David had been in an excellent mood for the past few days. No matter what Hannah suggested, he agreed enthusiastically. The editing work he'd done was some of the best in their two-year career. Both in terms of quantity and quality, he caught up on a month of backlogged content and their interaction numbers exploded.

Hannah attributed it to rest, real relaxation in a proper bed. Begrudgingly, she admitted her own sleep improved by having a luxurious bed to herself.

They plowed into the work headfirst, interviewing anyone who'd stop long enough to share the history of their village and their excitement about the upcoming harvest festival. At this rate, David explained, they might have enough content for full documentaries on both Sundebrennen and Maistadt with a weekly stream diving deep into the minor aspects of both.

Maistadt's founding could be traced all the way back to Columbus's return from the Americas. A few kernels of corn proved a bumper crop for the region and soon replaced all the standard grain staples. Farms extended outward, choking out any attempt at nearby settlements. This double-edged sword left the village cut off from greater Europe but maintained long-standing traditions that hadn't survived modernization elsewhere.

The people reminded Hannah of Amish or Mennonites back home, except these people were pleasant and happy. They had no issues with modern conveniences.

Sundebrennen, however, was the focus of this expedition.

As far as the neighbors (if you could call them neighbors) were concerned, the celebration had never been documented, written or otherwise. It was supposed to be an eerie festival where the locals built gigantic bonfires; wild dancing, endless laughing, and drunken singing throughout the night and late into the morning.

Maistadt-ians held to a deeper, spiritual interpretation.

October was the month of renewal. A season of remembrance, both of loved ones gone beyond the veil and previous decisions made. For the Maistadt natives, it seemed to be one last chance for absolution. Sins over the past year could, with this ritual, be wiped clean.

Sundebrennen, loosely translated from German as "Burning of Sins", consisted of several interconnected rituals which occurred on consecutive days leading up to the great forgiveness. The first was a city-wide march through the cornfields to ensure that no ears went to waste. Any unpicked ears of corn were considered sacred, chosen by the land itself to propagate the field. They were returned with much fanfare and placed in piles within wreaths of evergreen boughs and sprinkled with sacrificial sheep blood. Any animal would do, but the simple white wool was considered pure, and therefore preferable.

During the following week, the citizens cut, bundled, and stacked the stalks in great bales. Next came a day of rest and reflection. Each person spent 24 hours contemplating the mistakes and regrets of the past thirteen months, using a pre-Gregorian lunar calendar, then writing them down on strips of paper. These were then placed inside the scarecrows, called Strohpuppe. On the final day, the Strohpuppe would be stacked against a ziggurat of corn stalks and put to the torch. The concept was obvious, even to outsiders, by admitting and burning mistakes of the past, one could move into the new year with a blameless soul.

Of course, to make the ritual truly worthwhile, debauchery was not only acceptable, but encouraged. Drunkenness and fornication ran rampant. Often multiple partners joined one another, switching lovers with reckless abandon. Good natured fights would break out only for the combatants to shake hands and wipe bloodied noses. Theft, strangely, seemed entirely absent. Perhaps it was due to the strong sense of community.

David and Hannah were allowed to join in the festivities. Dozens of women offered themselves to him while dozens more made passes at Hannah. Both refused, though a particularly handsy fellow needed physical deterrence.

rite of passage for them to witness the frequent copulation, but neither David nor Hannah felt it was their place to put an end to it.

The night before the festival, Hannah decided to shatter the cold wall between them. He came after her with a renewed vigor and stamina, unmatched in two full years. Her screams must have been audible, because their door swung open. He was behind her, hair wrapped in one first, both facing the only entrance or exit.

Helga casually strolled in wearing nothing but a mischievous smirk.

"Might I choin in your fun? I can assure bozz uff you reach satisfaction."

How she rolled her R's into something closer to a W sent a tingle down David's spine. Before his mind had a chance to realize its error, caught up in the moment, he blurted his thoughts.

"Come on in! We could use a little spice."

Hannah bristled beneath him, and he realized just how badly he'd fucked up.

She whirled, breaking his grip and shoving him hard against the headboard.

"Are you fucking kidding me, right now? You pig!" Then, rounding on Helga, she erupted. "NO! You're not welcome. Bounce your tits somewhere else, you blonde bimbo bitch! Get! The fuck! OUT!"

Looking terrified, Helga slipped out, not bothering to close the door.

That left David as the sole target of Hannah's rage.

"I should have known better. You're just like every other guy I've ever dated, thinking with your stupid cock. Idiot! Fucking moron! You'll NEVER share my bed again. I hope it was worth it. Go enjoy your little skankwurst; turn her into a cream filled pretzel for all I care. I don't ever want to see you again!"

David stood, desperate to get a word in edgewise, suddenly filled with the overwhelming guilt of his nightly rendezvous.

Her verbal assault turned physical when he didn't move fast enough, and soon he was dodging shoes, pillows, and anything else she could lift. When she raised the chair, embers bursting into flame in her eyes, he slammed the door just in time. A loud thud followed along with an incoherent parade of screaming insults.

Heart sinking, he pulled up his trousers. They were all he managed to snatch.

Opening the door to his room, he found Helga, now wearing a bathrobe and sitting on his bed. Her cheeks ran with streaming mascara.

He slumped beside her. "You should probably go."

"I'm so sorry. It izn't your vay. Zingks are different here. I had nein intention off... off..." She sobbed, head slipping into his lap.

Not even that could rouse his broken enthusiasm.

Awkwardly, he patted her head, trying not to notice what had slipped out of her robe. "It's not your fault. It was mine. We have fights like this sometimes. Never this bad, but she'll cool off by morning. You should probably avoid her, though. I can't imagine we'll be here much longer anyway. I'm so sorry you got caught up in this. We really shouldn't have... done what we did."

"I don't regret anyzzinkt. Ve boss needed someone." She kissed his forehead, wiping her eyes, but not bothering to fix her robe as she left. "Zzank you fur ze memories."

David fell back on his bed. What had he done?

About an hour later, Hannah's door slowly creaked open. Her tears fell on her phone. She intended to delete every last picture of them.

"It's customary to bringkt a gift ven beggingkt forgiveness." She offered one of two pewter mugs of wine, which Hannah took absently.

When she didn't react violently, Helga sat beside her. She'd changed back into her serving attire with a notably less revealing undershirt.

"I'm not mad at you. I'm pissed at him. The whole situation. He's

Helga took a small sip of her own cup before pulling Hannah gently against her chest and rocking in a surprisingly motherly embrace.

"Husch mein fraulein. Time heals all vounds. Until zen, drink helps us forget."

Hannah drained the mug and let her sorrow soak Helga's shirt.

Soon, she was exhausted. Eyelids puffy and heavy, mind slowing to a glacial crawl.

"Sleep child, undt know peace."

She drifted off with Helga still in the room.

The following morning, Hannah was nowhere to be seen. David checked her room and found it empty. The bed was made, and the floor was clean, ready for the next guest.

Downstairs, the Tavernmaster claimed he hadn't seen her. He walked the short distance to their car, which was gone. That was all he needed to see to understand the gravity of his situation. She was ignoring his texts and unanswered calls went to voicemail. He left half a dozen before giving up. She was gone and he had to accept it.

Helga found him at one of the tables and offered a stein of beer.

"On ze house. Fur ze troubles." She said, giving him a sidelong hug.

After chasing the first with a second, he decided to make the best of things and joined in the celebration. His heart wasn't in it, but his mind needed the distraction.

Helga never left his side, encouraging and instructing him on how to prepare. He bought a new outfit, one befitting the setting and even wrote his sins on a bit of paper. It was thick, rough parchment like the papyrus he'd handled in Egypt. She advised that speaking future manifestations to the straw dolls would make them come true.

A line of people carried scarecrows to the pyre, quietly mumbling to them before tossing them in with the rest. He added his whispering, "New beginnings start now. A new life. A new me.”

Helga added her own and took his hand, guiding him back to the circle of citizens ringing the pile of straw, Strohpuppe, and written regrets.

The lamplighter, in full regalia as he'd been the night they'd met him, stepped forward with his lighting pole held proudly to the sky. Helga translated the German into David's ear.

“Forgiveness through flame. Absolution and rebirth.”

David repeated the words in their native tongue with the others.

As the candle fell, Helga kissed him, first his cheek, then his lips. Fire devoured the dry fuel, swirling up and around until the heat bordered unbearable. Songs rose, words he didn't understand, but he found himself lost in the stunning woman before him.

Maybe he could stay here a while longer? Get a job and enjoy the simple way of living for a bit. Long enough to figure out who he was and what he really wanted from life.

***

Hannah blinked away the deep fog clinging to her brain. She tried to spit out the rough texture in her mouth, but it wouldn't budge. Her arms felt like lead, but even if they hadn't been, she found them impossible to move. Her wrists ached against the tight string binding them to a wooden pole across her shoulders. Her ankles complained of the same. Slowly, her vision sharpened, and she looked out through stalks of corn piled on top of her. Eventually, she realized there were scarecrows, and she was dressed as they were. A pair of them stared back at her with painted black, judgmental eyes.

In the distance, she saw the lamplighter coming closer. Terror burst through her paralysis, and she tried to scream, but the wad of paper and corn husks drank in the sound, leaving no audible noise.

With wide eyed helplessness, she watched the flames grow, and heard the foreign words. She made out Helga and David in the crowd and struggled choked screams of agony as the smoke and fire found her flesh.

Hannah would never know whose hand had placed the gag or that, among what was written upon the parchment, were Helga's sins. David's name had been scrawled more than a dozen times, each circled with looping, elegant hearts. Hannah's own name appeared only once, beside the word "Mord".

And she burned.

Bert Lestrange's works include various degrees of Horror, Fantasy, Weird Fiction, and, occasionally, unadulterated Smut. He is the husband of Marie Lestrange, world traveler, and self-proclaimed foodie—though he has a weakness for gast station chilli dogs. He and his family's roots spiderweb across the mountains of East Tennessee. Caregiver, father, and proud ally.

Nicest asshole you'll ever meet.

THE SCREAMING HOUSE

CHRISTOPHER RIDGE AND DAVID E. ANDERSON

"That house screams," Chad said.

He and his friend, Tony, stood on the sidewalk staring at the Victorian-style house surrounded by a dry, rotted picket fence.

They were watching the trick-or-treaters as they ran from house to house, screaming and growling, all dressed up as monsters and ghosts. Plus, it was a great time to hit up a few neighborhood wiener roasts for free food. There was a block party from six to nine every year. Hot dogs, brats and s'mores wafted through the cool fall air.

Maybe steal some kid's candy.

Rough a couple up.

"What do you mean?" Tony asked.

"I mean, I can hear it scream late at night while I'm lying in bed." Chad lived next door.

"Do your mom and dad hear it?"

"I asked them, and they said no. But their room is on the far side of the house. My window is right there." He pointed. "I hear everything."

"I never see anybody come in or out of that house."

"Somebody lives there. Trust me."

The old Victorian-style house had flaking white paint and hanging gutters in the front. The front left window had a shutter missing, and the right window had a hole, as if it had been broken by a rock a long time ago.

"I don't think so," said Tony, pointing at the grass. "Nobody's cut this lawn in years. You can get lost walking in these weeds."

"The screams ain't all I hear. I also hear doors slamming. Like coming from the back."

Tony thought for a moment, then grinned. "Let's go check it out."

Chad shook his head vigorously. "No way, dude. You're nuts. I ain't going back there."

"C'mon. It'll be fun."

"It's too dark."

"Scared of the dark, are you?" Tony punched him in the shoulder playfully.

"I'm not. It's just...there's something seriously wrong with this house."

Chad went on to explain how the small, narrow windows look like eyes, and with the way the door frame is tilted, it made it look like the house was laughing.

"Laughing?"

"Dude. I'm serious. Just look at it."

Tony bit his lower lip and cradled his chin in thumb and forefinger as if studying. "I don't see nothing but an old, rickety house that's one good wind gust away from falling down. I mean, look at those missing boards on the side, and the wood porch looks like it's going to collapse. I'm surprised the town hasn't condemned it."

"I wish they would."

"Hey, I got an idea."

Chad lowered his head. "Ohhh, no."

"I haven't even said what the idea is."

"Your ideas are never good."

"Just because something's a bad idea doesn't mean it won't be a good time."

"Fine, what's your idea?"

"Let's dare a trick-or-treater to walk up to the house and knock on the door. Then we'll know someone is there."

"But I know someone is there. I hear the screams."

"You may think you're hearing screams. Maybe you're just hearing the wind."

"That's what my dad said. Every little sound I hear, he says it's the wind, as if it's all normal and shit."

Tony sighed. "I'm just saying. It could be anything."

"Dude. I know what I hear." He grabbed his hat as a gust of wind practically blew it off. He tightened the collar on his jacket.

"Maybe you're hearing a ghost."

A trick-or-treater with an orange bag and wearing a black cape and Scream mask was running toward them, hacking the air with a slasher knife.

"Hey, kid," said Tony, grabbing the boy's shoulder as he ran past, stopping him in his tracks.

The kid jabbed the knife into Tony's arm with a shout, but of course the knife was only plastic, so it did no damage. "Let go of me, you perv!"

"Come on, man," said Chad. "No."

Tony ignored his friend. "I'm not gonna hurt you. What's your name, kid?"

"I don't give my name to pervs."

"I'm not a perv. My name's Tony. This is Chad. I'm just wondering if you're up for...an adventure." Tony let go of him.

"What's in it for me?" said the kid, puffing up his chest.

"Like I said, it's an adventure. There's an adventure in it for you. Cool, right?"

The kid shook his head and started walking away.

"Ten bucks," said Tony. "I'll pay you ten bucks."

"Ten bucks?" The kid turned and removed his mask, revealing a red-haired kid with a chubby, freckled face. "Let me see it."

"Sure." Tony pulled out his wallet and opened it. He looked inside and pulled two bills. His face fell. He turned to Chad. "I only have six bucks on me. Can you..."

"Absolutely not. This is a terrible idea."

The kid walked up and snatched the two bills, stuffing them into his pocket. "My name's Dennis. What do you want me to do?"

"Just go up to the house and knock on the door. See who answers."

"That old house? No one lives there," said Dennis.

"You live around here?" asked Chad.

Dennis nodded.

"Do you ever see anything happening here at this house? Or...hear anything?"

Dennis shook his head.

"Just go up and knock," said Tony.

"I don't have to go inside or anything?"

"Nope. Just knock and see if anyone answers."

"Why don't you guys just do it?"

"We would, but my friend's a total chicken-shit."

Chad gave Tony a dirty look, and Tony laughed.

"Pussies," said Dennis, putting his mask back on. He pushed on the metal gate, which fell off its rusty hinges, crashing to the walkway. He stepped over the gate and walked carefully up the rotted wooden steps, looking down at the porch as if worried it wouldn't hold him. He took a few big, slow steps, testing each board, eventually putting himself at the front door.

Dennis looked back to make sure the guys were still watching, then turned back and pounded on the front door. He lifted his orange plastic bag, and held it open in two hands. "Trick or—"

With a loud crack, the porch floor gave way beneath him, and Dennis crashed through, disappearing from sight.

"Shit!" Tony ran up, climbing the stairs, but was afraid to step onto the porch.

Chad was more hesitant, but moved forward. He was afraid of the house, yes, but was more worried about what had happened to Dennis. The kid wasn't yelling for help, which could mean he wasn't hurt, but it could also mean he was dead—perhaps impaled on a board with a rusty nail through the back of his head.

He looked around to see if anyone else was coming, but there was no one in the immediate area, and those he could see further away didn't seem to have heard anything. He approached the porch, but stopped at the bottom of the stairs.

"Where is he?" asked Chad.

Tony stepped forward onto the porch to better see through the hole Dennis had disappeared through. "I don't see him, man."

Tony screamed down the hole for Dennis.

"Dude, where is he?" Chad asked.

"He's got to be down here somewhere." He screamed for his name again. expecting to hear something at least. "Deeeeeennis!"

"Dude. This is so not good." Chad ran his fingers through his hair. "I told you something was up with this house."

"Hey, we both agreed to dare someone to knock on the door."

"I never agreed, dude. It was all you."

Tony shrugged. "Whatever. He has to be down there, right? He's probably crawling out from under the porch somewhere."

"I don't think so." Chad wished he'd never mentioned anything about the house to Tony.

"Well, he couldn't have gone far, that's for sure." Tony swiped the phone screen and turned on the flashlight. He leaned over the hold as far down as he could, and shined the light.

"See anything?"

"Just gravel. Oops, and a rat just ran past."

"Gross. What are we going to do now?"

"I have no idea. Just wait for him to show up somewhere?"

"What are you looking for?" A young kid walked up, dressed in a suit and wearing black-rim glasses, holding a trick-or-treat bag.

Chad turned. "Nothing."

"Then why are you looking down the hole in the porch of a haunted house?"

Tony stood, brushing the dirt off his jeans. "We thought we heard something. Aren't you supposed to be trick or treating?" He was hoping to distract the nosey little snot in hopes of getting him to go away.

The kid tilted his head and smirked. "The house swallowed somebody, didn't it?"

Chad scrunched his eyebrows. "What?"

"It swallowed somebody."

"We thought we heard something." Chad leaned over further, trying to get a glimpse of Dennis.

"My dad told me not to get close to that house. He says it's dangerous and hurts people."

"We're fine," Tony said. "Now, just fuck the hell off and get more candy, youngster. Capisce?"

The kid glared at him. "You're asking for trouble, you realize."

"We're okay, kid. Seriously."

The door squeaked on its rusty hinges as it opened. Tony yelped, and the door slammed shut.

Chad looked up from the hole, and Tony was gone.

He quickly backed away from the door and jumped off the porch, yelling for Tony.

No answer.

"Tooooony!"

"I told you," the kid said. "I'm telling my daddy."

Chad raised his hands. "No. Don't do that yet. We don't want to scare anybody. I'm sure he's here...somewhere."

The kid shook his head. "Nope. It swallowed him."

"Obviously he went in the house."

"People that go inside don't come out. That's what my dad says. He says it's been that way for a long, long time."

Chad climbed back onto the porch, stepped over the hole, grabbed the large brass handle, and pressed the latch on top.

Locked.

"Hey, Kid—" began Chad, but he turned, and the kid was gone. For a moment, he feared the house had taken him, but then saw him booking through the broken gate, leaving Chad alone with the house.

What should I do?

He didn't want to leave when the house had Tony and that Dennis kid. He knew that if he just fled, he'd be overwhelmed with guilt.

But neither did he want to go inside. To get swallowed up like they did.

People who go inside don't come out.

But how could he go in if the door was locked? If the house wanted to keep him out, it would keep him out. Not much he could do about that.

He realized that he believed the house had a will of its own.

But maybe...

He gripped the door handle tight and closed his eyes. "Please," he said. "May I come in?" He wasn't sure he meant it, wasn't sure he'd go inside even if the house let him. But he had to know.

He felt a click, and the latch descended under his thumb. Surprised, he let go and stepped back, his heel finding the edge of the hole in the porch. The front door slowly opened with a loud creak.

He took a deep swallow and stepped forward, his left foot crossing the door's threshold.

"CHAD!" he heard a voice scream. Tony's voice. It was so loud, he assumed people could hear it for blocks, but he turned and saw a family of five walking down the sidewalk past the house, all dressed as a smorgasbord of superheroes. The youngest, dressed as Batman, rode in a stroller, bouncing excitedly, and the parents talked to the older kids. They clearly hadn't heard the scream. It was in Chad's head only.

"SAVE ME!" Tony screamed. "I'M HERE! I'M INSIDE! PLEASE, CHAD! FOR THE LOVE OF GOD, SAVE ME!"

Then another voice called out. "HELP! HELP! GET ME OUT OF HERE!" It was Dennis.

Chad tried to place the direction of the voices, but couldn't. They didn't seem to be coming from inside the house, not really. It was as if they came from the house itself, like the house was speaking in their voices. Was he really hearing Tony and Dennis, or was the house mimicking them?

"Where are you, Tony?" called Chad.

"I'M IN THE BASEMENT! IT'S SO DARK DOWN HERE! HELP ME!"

"You're not Tony!" yelled Chad. He turned away from the door, preparing to leap over the hole and flee the house.

The remaining floorboards on the patio suddenly rose under Chad's feet, flinging him backward through the open front door. He landed on his back, hitting the wooden floor hard and knocking the breath out of him.

He looked up at the door, watching it slam shut in front of him, and he knew he was screwed.

Chad found himself lying on his back, gasping for air. He was lying in what looked like a large living room foyer. There was a Victorian-style cabinet by the door.

There were paintings on the walls. He blinked hard several times, trying to get his vision to clear and to regroup his thoughts.

He saw the picture in front of him was that of what had to be somebody's great great grandfather. The man was dressed in a suit and holding a hatchet in his hand. The hatchet's blade was soaked in blood.

The picture to the right of this was of an old woman, possibly the other man's wife. She was holding a naked, headless baby by its feet. The baby's arms were dangling as blood dripped from its neck.

He wondered what the hell kind of old-time pictures these were. He'd never seen anything like them before.

This house was sick.

He heard footsteps. Not solid footsteps, but more like someone shuffling.

Grunting.

Groaning and heavy breathing.

He heard screaming. The screaming sounded like Tony.

A pair of dirty bare feet with large, filthy, fungus-ridden toenails stopped at his head. The legs were hairy, as wide as a small tree trunk.

The man's face came into view as it looked down on him. Smiling a tar-yellow stained smile with two missing front teeth. His hair was long and oily, and his arms were covered in dirt. Blood was all over his fingers. His face was deformed, lopsided, one eye bigger than the other and his mouth wider on one side. He wore filthy, torn overalls with no shirt beneath.

The man grunted and slapped his chest as if he were excited that he captured yet more prey.

"Please," Chad said. He gulped, his throat suddenly dry. "Please don't hurt me. We meant no harm." He knew it was a stupid thing to say, but it was still worth a shot.

He heard Tony and the kid screaming. It sounded like it was coming from a room somewhere down the long hallway.

The screaming must have excited the man because he jumped up and down like he was a five-year-old full of excitement on Christmas morning.

He slapped his chest with two fists like a gorilla.

He grabbed Chad by his feet with his left hand. His hand was almost the size of Chad's head and easily wrapped around both feet. He pulled Chad down the long hallway, toward the screaming.

Chad kicked and wiggled, trying to free himself from the vice-like clutches of this man. But he was no match for the brute's strength, dragged behind what he was saying?

He looked around for Tony and Dennis and saw...well, he didn't know what he saw, exactly. There they were, side-by-side in the wall, their eyes glazed over as if dead, the kid without his Scream mask. He couldn't tell if they were breathing. And Chad couldn't wrap my mind around what became of their bodies.

The walls seemed to be growing through them. Not like they were impaled on the boards or anything, more like they'd been standing there and someone built the wall through them. Impossible, of course, as they'd been outside with Chad only a few minutes earlier. It was like...their bodies just became one with the wall. Became part of the house. Absorbed.

He still heard Tony scream, but his friend's mouth wasn't moving and just hung there. It was his voice, but it wasn't coming from him.

"CHAD! SAVE ME!" Tony yelled, but it wasn't Tony. It was the house, showing Chad the method it had used to draw him into its trap. It had spent weeks trying to lure him in with an unfamiliar scream, but that hadn't been enough. But using Tony and that Dennis kid had done the trick.

Then the brute standing above him grabbed a meat cleaver from a knife rack, bringing it down on Chad's right hand, severing it in half.

Chad screamed, even louder than he'd screamed so far, and watched his upper hand and the attached four fingers come free, and blood sprayed from the open wound across the madman's body. The brute threw his head back and laughed. He brought the cleaver down again, this time onto Chad's wrist, taking off the whole hand in one blow, and yet more blood sprayed, an artery having opened.

The cleaver kept coming down. Onto his chest. His stomach. Onto his throat. His head. It wasn't long before Chad was mercifully dead, his blood leaking off the counter onto the kitchen floor, then disappearing as the house absorbed his blood into itself.

But the screaming didn't stop. No, it certainly did not.

That old Victorian home bordered two houses, you see. Chad's to the west and another house to the east.

Inside that house, fourteen-year-old Julie Baymont was eating her assortment of Halloween candy while thumbing through a Nancy Drew mystery. She heard a young man's screams coming from the old Victorian house next door. She initially shrugged it off as some kid playing a Halloween prank, but when it went on and on, she brought her parents to her room. They heard nothing, and told her she was imagining things.

No, I'm not, she thought.

She asked herself what Nancy Drew would do in this situation.

Go and investigate, right?

Christopher Ridge is a writer of the gross, grotesque and the nasty. He writes anything from creature features, ghosts to crazed psychos. Psychopath tales are his favorite though. His stories tend to be brutal, gory with some dark humor splashed in.

His stories have been published in an anthology edited by Jim Goforth in his Rejected for Content series titled The Sanitarium. Also the splatterpunk anthology Guts and Gore. His story The Sea Wolves was recently picked up by The Horror Zines Book of Werewolf Stories with Ramsey Campbell and Nancy Kilpatrick along with many others.

He is an exterminator by day and writer in the early morning and late evening hours. He lives in Indianapolis Indiana with his wife and two sons.

David E. Anderson grew up in the '70s, loving Godzilla movies and the "Night Stalker" series, developing a love for horror early on. As a teenager, he immersed himself in the books by the likes of Stephen King, F. Paul Wilson and Dean Koontz, and wanted to try his hand at what they do so well. He wrote his first novel, "The Void," in his mid-teens, followed by six more—three of which he's self-published.

THE CAULDRON

L.W. Young

"Trick or treat!" I cried, holding out the plastic bag.

The look on the man's face as he opened the door almost sent me running home. I'd later find out that he, Jarvis Brown, had been merely 19 years old when the incident that would change both our lives took place. He looked enough like a man, he had the same tired, small, and black rimmed eyes that I remember seeing on my dad whenever he came back from the factory. Jarvis's eyes were faintly hidden by hanging strands of greasy hair which might have been blonde at one point.

"Tr... trick or treat?" I repeated, my Batman costume now feeling very ineffectual.

Jarvis just stared at me with a long, dopey smile.

"Where are your friends?" he asked softly.

Lowering the bag, I reached from my inhaler and took a big gulp. Mum didn't let me have many friends. Earlier that evening, when the other kids at school had been chatting about going trick or treating this evening, I hadn't even bothered asking them if I could join them. The only reason I was out here on my own, secretly defying Mum's orders, was to prove that nothing bad would happen to me. So far, it was going well...

"Are..." I trembled, trying to appear tough, "are you going to give me some candy or what?"

Jarvis's smile widened.

"Oh?" his eyes sparkled, "Batman's threatening me, huh?"

I said nothing. Hunkering down to my eye level, Jarvis lay a greasy hand on my shoulder and pulled me towards him, making me squirm.

"Listen little guy, I used to have no friends just like you," Jarvis told me, that slippery smile glued to his face, "so, I decided to throw a special Halloween party tonight and invite everyone I know. Can't you hear how much fun we're having?"

All I could hear coming from inside the house was the machine gun din of thrash metal music. I was still standing with the bag held out like an idiot as I listened, completely forgetting what I'd even come here for.

"How about it, little dude?" the smile grew longer on his face, "want to come in and join us?"

Refusing to accept invitations from strangers was the one piece of advice which I resoundingly agreed with my mother on, so I squeezed my lips shut and shook my head.

Then, Jarvis pulled out a knife.

I dropped the bag and reeled, my heart hammering. Suddenly, the red splotches on his worn-out Metallica shirt looked like more than just pizza stains.

"Oh, don't worry buddy! It's only part of my costume," he laughed, pulling an embarrassed face, "I'm a serial killer, see? Boo!"

"W... why would your Mum let you dress like that?" was all I could think to ask.

His lips pulled back to reveal a long row of yellow teeth.

"Because I'm a grown up," he told me, "And this is my grown-up party."

Grownups had parties at home and not at Chuck E. Cheese? How miserable.

"We've got plenty of candy, as well as beer, music..." his bloodshot eyes then flashed me a wink, "and even girls."

With his hand still gripping my shoulder, I looked around the lamp lit neighborhood. There were two cars in the driveway, and plenty of people walking up and down the street in costumes with adults watching over them. Inside his house, however, I'd be all alone. Moreover, Mum didn't know where I was.

"Unless, of course," Jarvis mused, picking his teeth with the knife, "you're a chicken."

Jarvis bent his skinny arms into wings and started flapping them at me, balking like an idiot. Even at the age of ten, I should have been above such a taunt, but my attitude was tied to a deep-rooted certainty: after tonight, Mum would never let me go out like this again. If she was around, I couldn't imagine being allowed to go to grown-up parties even by the time I reached 35. However, even if I only went inside Jarvis's house for a couple of seconds, I'd have something to brag about once I got back to school. How many of the other boys in elementary school could honestly brag about hanging out with a girl at a grown-up party? They might even have a reason to finally like me.

"O... okay, fine," I shrugged as if I'd been to tons of adult parties before, "why not."

I brushed past Jarvis into the house, and I heard him lock the front door behind us.

Walking into the hallway, I was hit by a rancid smell.

"What is that?" I faltered, rushing my hands to my nose.

"Oh, that's the dog," Jarvis snorted from behind me, herding me into the front room, "he shits everywhere."

Passing the kitchen, I briefly saw pots and pans piled up in the sink, and split rubbish bags gathered by the backdoor. From the garden came the barking of a mad bloodhound, which even made the flimsy garden door shudder in its frame.

"Shut up!" Jarvis yelled while pushing me into the living room, "fucking dog!"

Jarvis then shoved me into the party room where the music blared. The room was lit by candles glowing inside the mouths of various decaying pumpkins from around the room. Jarvis hadn't been lying about having friends, there were three bodies sprawled out on the moldy sofas, all of them about Jarvis's age. I might have only been a kid, but even I could tell they were all high on something.

"I just need to check on the mutt," Jarvis massaged my shoulders, "I'll just leave you kids to get acquainted, adios!"

He slapped me on the shoulders, making me jump, and departed. I was left standing alone with three strangers in the musty room, holding my empty shopping bag out like a shield.

"Um, hi..." I attempted with a wave.

The teens groaned, seemingly oblivious to my presence. There were empty bottles and cans on every surface, which can't have all been from this evening. The only other sound in the room was the hum of the fish tank against the far wall where a few Koi Carp were floating belly up.

Then, I noticed something which made the pit fall out of my stomach. I dropped the bag, splashing candy all over the floor as my hands shot up to my mouth.

I realized that, jutting through the face of the boy sitting nearest to me wearing skinny jeans and a red t-shirt, was a bloody razor blade. The blade had been pushed up through his palate, tearing a bloody hole in the gap between his nose and mouth, where it hung like a botched piercing. The boy was clearly in agony, but his hands lay limply at his sides, twitching. His eyes turned on me, watching me in a haze. He then choked, coughing a fountain of crimson down his face. If this get up was part of some kind of costume, he should be working for Hollywood.

The second boy, slumped with his face in the first kid's crotch, had his eyes clenched in pain. There was burning, puffy skin all over his face, clearly inflamed by some sort of rash. He was a big guy with wide shoulders and a tight-fitting tank top, so whatever Jarvis had done to him must have caught him by surprise.

The third-party member was indeed a girl. She was a tall, slender girl with her small head, flame orange hair tied up in a bun, and cherub nose facing the ceiling, staring at the motionless fan blades with vacant eyes. To me, her pasty white make-up, black lipstick, fishnet sleeves and platform shoes made her look like some kind of street mime. Save for the warts and ulcers building up in the corners of her mouth, she was quite beautiful. Her right arm lay out on the sofa, clutching a half bitten red apple. Rattling breath heaved up from her throat as she sat motionless on her chair, her lungs fighting for life. I recognised her symptoms immediately; she was having an allergic reaction. They all were.

Then I saw the cauldron in the centre of the room, propped between the two sofas. This wasn't some plastic prop from the local Walmart, it was a fat, iron bowl flecked with rust which took up practically half of the living room. Wisps of steam floated off the surface, seeming to curl into the shape of a finger and call me over to it.

Spellbound, I went. Standing up on my tiptoes, I peered over the side. The cauldron was full of floating red blobs, bloody water, and razor blades. As I leaned in closer, a floating tongue bobbed to the surface, sticking out at me.

I reeled. Before I had a chance to scream, a voice called out to me.

"Help... help..."

It was the girl. I turned around and saw her, reaching out to me with a pale, shaking hand wrapped in its frilly black sleeve. Her head stuck to the back rest; she was too weary to move it.

"Are you all right?" I gasped, racing up next to her on the sofa.

Stupid question, I know, but I was a kid, alright? She managed a tired smile as I sat on my knees on the cushion beside her. She then burst into a coughing fit, launching flecks of blood on her mouth.

"Listen to me..." Shirley croaked through her swollen throat, "you... have... to call... an ambulance..."

She started coughing again.

"What did he do to you?" I asked, now painfully aware of the danger I was in.

"Jarvis... poisoned us..." she slurred.

It didn't take long for me to conclude that 'Jarvis' was our fabulous host.

"How?" I sat up, tugging at her frilly black top.

The girl waved a finger towards the iron cauldron.

"He put something toxic... in the water..." she managed, "and... razor blades... in some of the apples..."

With a gasp, I finally realized that the red blobs I had seen in the cauldron were actually apples, simple store-bought apples.

"Why?" I begged her, tears stirring in my eyes.

"Because..." she croaked, gently peeling my hands away, and staring through me with her black-rimmed, bloodshot eyes, "we... tried to be... his friends..."

The answer made no sense to me. It still doesn't...

The girl's breathing became hoarser and more strained as the blotches on her lips started to inflate in the same way mine did once when I got too close to an open jar of peanut butter. That was when I remembered the two EpiPens in my belt pouch which my Mum made me take everywhere I went. Fumbling with the zip on the front of my Batman utility belt, I whipped out the EpiPen and snapped off the top.

"This will make it all better," I approached her with the needle, doing my best impression of Mum, "just be brave now..."

"No!" she coughed, using all her strength to motion to where the two boys were sitting, "give it... to... THEM!"

I shot a glance at the other two victims, one whose face was still bleeding badly, the other who was lying face down and not breathing. The girl was right, they both looked in a lot worse shape than her, but I didn't have enough shots for everyone. The big lad must have taken a dose of the poison first and looked too far gone. As for the other one, an adrenaline shot wasn't exactly going to fix the gaping hole in his face, was it? I looked back at the dying girl.

To this day, I still wonder what it was that stopped me from doing as she asked. Was it because I had simply reached her first, or was it because she was a female? From what little my tiny ten-year-old brain understood; males were people who went out to the factory one day and never came back or went on Halloween adventures to stranger's houses only to find themselves caught in a death game. Female meant mother. Female meant safety. Female means 'will always be there'. Was I really going to ignore one of the boys just to save what a 'female' represented to my childish brain?

I'm sure Freud would have a field day over all this...

"Tsk, naughty naughty!" a voice laughed behind me, snapping me out of my thoughts, "I should have known better than to leave you with my girl!"

I turned. Jarvis was grinning maniacally down at me. I tried to flee, but he grabbed me in his big hands and locked my arms at their sides. His brute strength made me drop my EpiPen. Screaming, I ripped my hand out of his grasp and pulled away from him. My heart was hammering in my chest as he pinned me against the iron cauldron and pressed his knife against me.

"You hurt them," I whimpered, unable to look at anything but the approaching blade.

"You're a smart kid," he sneered.

"WHY!?"

"Because they deserved it."

"What about me?" I panicked, "do I deserve it too?"

"Probably," he sighed, "but don't worry, we're going to play a little game first..."

He lunged forward and wrapped his hands around my waist.

"What are you doing!?" I screamed as he hoisted me up into the air.

"Haven't you ever tried bobbing for apples?" Jarvis asked as he carried me, "come on kid, it's Halloween, you have to give it a try!"

"But you poisoned the water!" I struggled, "and the apples..."

"That's your problem," he laughed, dangling me over the cauldron.

I struggled for my life. The stench of the bloody, bubbling water rose up at me as Jarvis lowered me down. That's when I noticed that my yellow fanny pouch was still hanging open with the remaining EpiPen caught in the zipper, about to slip away from me. Just in time, I grabbed it in my free hand and flipped the end off with my thumb (Mum had taught me how to do it with only one hand). Twisting around, I jabbed the needle into Jarvis's neck and pressed down on the plunger.

"Argh!" he grunted as he dropped me, feeling for the lump of plastic now sticking out of his neck, "what!?"

"Trick or treat," I yelled in his face, suddenly feeling like a total badass, "a... ASSHOLE!"

Howling, he dropped me. As I went down, my sneakers caught on the edge of the cauldron, toppling it, and spilling reddened water, rep apples, and chunks of bloody flesh across the living room floor. Sitting up quickly, I kept my mouth and nose away from the stuff, clambering up onto the sofa like I was playing an all too real game of 'the floor is lava'. Hugging myself against Shirley, who was now too far gone to stay awake, I watched my attacker from atop the sofa. He was splashing around on the drenched carpet as the apples washed up at his sides. I watched him clawing at his throat as he rolled over, a knot of bulging purple veins popping up at the point where I'd just stabbed him.

Approaching the girl, I fished the second EpiPen out of my front pocket.

"No..." I heard her mutter as I jabbed the pen into her leg, tearing a hole in her stockings.

It was too late. The syringe was already empty.

With my heart thudding in my chest, I collapsed into the stinky sofa. The carpet seemed to be smoking from whatever toxic substance Jarvis had laced it with and brought with it a stench of burning plastic which was almost preferable to the moldy smell of the whole house. The boombox which had been playing heavy metal music fizzed out as the water swamped its circuitry. Below me, Jarvis had stopped thrashing around and was now merely gasping like a dying fish as his eyes rolled back into their sockets as he lay on the ground.

Opposite me, Shirley's two friends were now slumped together on the couch like spooning lovers, utterly motionless.

I started to cry. What the hell was I supposed to do now? That's when I heard Mum's voice in my head telling me to be a "brave little soldier", willing me onto my feet. Climbing over Shirley's comatose body, leaving the needle stuck in her leg, I stomped across the sofa and made a dash for the kitchen. Traversing the strange house, I used the grease-stained walls for support while I sought out a telephone.

The rotting stench of the kitchen slowed me down as I battled my way through clouds of hovering flies to find one. Finally, I saw it mounted on the wall with its coiled line dangling above the remains of a rat lying belly up on the countertop. I made a dash for it when I heard snarling to the right of me. A sliver of ice ran down my spine. I realized I could now feel a cool breeze of the night air tickling the hairs on my neck. The dog was loose.

Standing on gaunt legs and guarding the telephone was the growling beast. The long-haired greyhound with mangy, had now looked up from burying its snout in the remains of a stinking, gutted bin bag, and now aimed its hungry yellow eyes at me. It bared a set of jagged teeth, snapping its jaws.

"Nice doggie..." I began, reaching for the phone.

As soon as I moved, it barked, snapping its teeth at me. Before I could retreat, its paws had skidded along the kitchen floor and it leapt on me, trapping me under its weight. Its fangs charged at my face.

But that was when a red sphere, about the size of a cricket ball, came hurtling through the air and slammed straight into the side of the hound's head with frightening accuracy. The animal made a helpless yelp before its body flopped down onto me. After a few seconds of dead silence, I was finally brave enough to peek out from my fingers and see the animal lying on top of me with its tongue lolling out of its mouth. From this close, I could see that the red ball sticking to the animal's forehead was an apple fitted with an outward sticking razor blade. The fruit had been thrown at the exact right angle to penetrate the animal's brain.

Raising my head, I looked up at my savior. It was Shirley, standing in the kitchen doorway in a pitcher's follow through stance, panting and sweating from the sudden shot of adrenaline administered by my EpiPen...

After that, we called the police.

The cops showed up and uncovered the rest of Jarvis Brown's house of horrors. His mother was found upstairs, slumped in her chair with the TV blaring in front of her. She'd been dead for days. After a particularly brutal shouting match (which neighbors claimed had been a regular event), Jarvis had laced her nightcap with PPD, the same toxic substance he'd spiked the cauldron with at the party.

PPD was a poisonous substance widely used to oxidize hair dye. Jarvis had been planning his little game for weeks, working out how he was going to lure classmates over to his house and trick them into ingesting the substance through a seemingly innocent game of apple bobbing. Once one of the unfortunate attendees had bitten into an apple which concealed a razor blade, it was already too late for all of them.

Accounts from his classmates said Jarvis always seemed like a troubled kid, which is why Shirley and her friends had taken pity on him when he'd invited them to his Halloween party. Little did they know of the horrors Jarvis had planned for them. Jarvis miraculously survived the encounter. To this day, I believe he's still institutionalized.

Shirley survived, but her two friends didn't. I heard that she felt responsible for what happened, but really it was my fault.

As for me, my Mum naturally gave me the grounding of my life when she found out her precious golden boy had defied her strict order for one day and almost gotten himself killed in Ted Bundy Jr's little murder house. However, that was until the press came calling to interview the 10-year-old hero who had managed to save one vulnerable girl from a deranged classmate. I was even asked to give a presentation about it at school where I was given a scripted list of advice to give to other kids if they were in similar danger and what could have happened if I'd just run away at the very start like I wanted to.

After that, Mum loosened up and took me out to theme park trips, parties, and even on overseas holidays. I think the whole experience made her feel that she couldn't keep me wrapped up in cotton wool forever lest something like this happen again.

She still calls me her brave little boy. But to this day, I remember how Shirley had pleaded with me to use the EpiPen on her friends instead of her, and I'm still not sure I believe it...

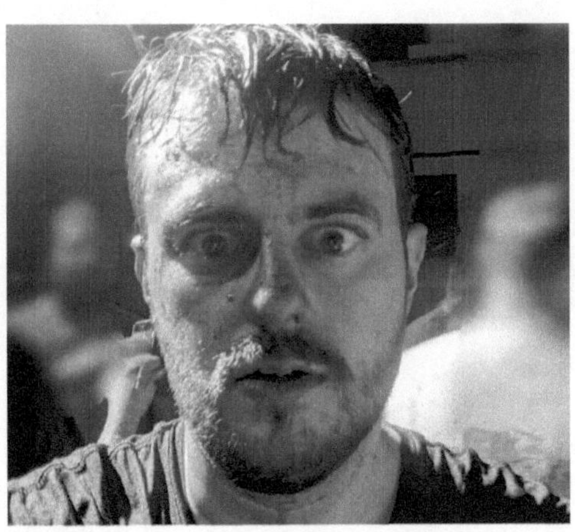

L.W. Young graduated from the University of Kent with a BA Honors degree in English literature and creative writing. He has experience with writing for theater, film and YouTube, and is a passionate advocate of mindfulness and raising awareness of mental health issues. His favourite authors and influences include an eclectic bag: ranging from Stephen King to Cormac McCarthy to Ray chandler to David Mitchell to Kazuyo Ishigoda to Margaret Atwood and Colson Whitehead. However, if you ask him, he would probably tell you his favourite books are the Point Horror novels he read in his High School library as a teenager.

HELL HATH COME TO DANDRUM

Marie Lestrange

"But I don't want to be a ghost again this year, Momma!" My little sister stamped her foot with all the force of a teddy bear, while simultaneously emitting the rage of a wild animal. Mother pursed her lips to prevent the smile that I could see attempting to burst through. She quickly looked at me and we both looked away, for fear of embarrassing the littlest among us by laughing at her miniscule might.

I knelt, gathering her sweet little hands in mine, scrunching my nose up and nuzzling it against hers, something that usually made her laugh. Tonight, she stood still as stone. "Now Emmy Loud, Momma and I tried and tried to help you find a different costume for this year." I raised my eyebrows, giving her the "mmmhm, you know big sissy's right" look. "I even offered to take you down to old man Joe's shop and take a look at the costumes he had in there! But you didn't wanna."

Emily sat on the floor with a huff, criss cross applesauce and an expression to match. "Those costumes are stinky, sissy, I wanted a bwand new one.

Even though she tried to hide it, I saw Mother's crestfallen face as she turned around and headed into the kitchen. She worked and scraped and prayed so hard for us, but after the coal mines took Daddy to stay with them forever (which is how we told Emily about it)...no sense in describing how he was crushed into an unrecognizable pulp from the cave in to her– there just wasn't enough money for extras like there used to be.

"Doesn't matter if you're dressed as a ghost or a witch or a scarecrow... we're still gonna have the best time ever!"

Emmy scowled and turned away. Now this just wouldn't do. I pulled off my witch hat and sat on the floor behind her, the crumpling plastic of my "costume" giving me away. Honestly, costume was giving it a ton of credit, because this year, just like the last and the last, I was dressed in a large black trash bag with only the witch hat to clue everyone in as to what I was.

"Emmy Lou, sweet baby..." her face softened as she looked up at mine, "Momma does her best to put food in our bellies and keep us living in this house, you hear me?" My sister's eyes welled up a little bit, eyes that had seen too many hardships in her mere five years. I continued, "We're lucky to get to go to the dance at all...and you know we're gonna have fun there no matter what!"

She nodded, picking at a bit of carpet that was slowly unraveling but God knows there weren't the funds to fix it. "But what if they make fun of me, Sissy? The other girls...in their pink princess costumes with tiaras and make up and those glittery sparkle shoes I saw at the Walmart that one time."

I sighed, pulling her into my lap and hugging tight. "Not a chance, little bug! Besides, a bedsheet ghost is the coolest vintage costume around! It's one of the first Halloween get ups people started to wear!"

"Really!?"

Aw. There it was. The little twinkle in her eyes had returned.

"Yep," I nodded, standing and pulling her to her feet to join me. "Besides, it's just one night! Now go on and git ready so we aren't late!" She scampered off down the hallway to pick out who knows what pattern of sheet to wear. We didn't have white ones, since the well water stained anything and everythang, but I would have a couple of my friends tell her how special and awesome her costume was to smooth things over once we got there.

Momma leaned on the doorframe and gave me a soft, warm smile that hardly reached her eyes.

"Thank you, Wendy."

I hugged her tight, trying my best to transfer some warmth and happiness to her and erase that creeping sadness that had taken hold after Daddy died. "Love you, Momma."

"Love you too, sweet girl."

***

Emmy Lou was off like a rocket as soon as we got there, immediately hitting the dance floor with her bestest buds, Lisa and Danny, the three musketeers of Dandrum. The banjos and guitars were awesome, they'd gone all out on the decorations this year, and Jessica had even brought a little no no corn juice to add to our punch cups and make this a really fun night (as she'd said).

"Nahhhh. None for me, sis, but thank you!" I placed a hand over my cup to prevent her from pouring any of the moonshine in.

"Ahhhhh come on, Wen! Let loose a little bit!" Jessica kept raising her eyebrows and nudging me, but I wasn't as easily persuaded as the others.

"Thanks sis, but you know I've got to get little bit home after this...next time! Next time, I promise!"

Jessica rolled her eyes, baring her "fangs" and hissed to announce her annoyance. A vampire through and through this evening, I chuckled.

After one two many rounds of line dancing, Jessica and I grabbed a couple of seats near the buffet. I almost laughed at the skeletal "charcoochie," as we liked to call them, with entrails of fresh mozzarella and pepperonis and a bunch of other fancy meats I didn't know, surrounded by a fresh cracker grave with fruit and veggie "flowers." Whoever from the city council put this together must have really put some thought into it. It was sweet.

"Howdy Doody Halloween Dancers!" The wail of a microphone too close to the speakers caused everyone to clap their hands over their ears as one.

The Mayor laughed, turning beet red as he stood on stage at the front of the room. "Uhhh whoops. Sorry about that ya'll. Ok. Ok. Where was I?" He wiped the dripping sweat from his forehead, and it was no wonder because the King cape and crown had to be hot as hell here in the boys and girls club.

"Oh yes! Halloween Dancers!" he bellowed. "It's about time for our annual Craaaaaazy Costume Contest!"

I almost felt sorry for him as you could've heard a pin drop at the announcement. He really had to try harder to rouse up this crowd after interrupting their dancing, it seemed.

43

"Well...what if I tell you the winner of the costume contest gets $500!!!"

$500!

What?

He can't be serious now, can he?

What in blue blazes is that man on about now?

The rumble of confusion swept through the room like those earthquakes we hear about. Don't have em' down here in the south, but I bet they're pretty scary. Anywhoo...I guess those words were exactly what everyone wanted to hear, because damn near the entire gymnasium filed in line to compete in the contest.

"Now, now," said the mayor, his hanky now drenched by the sweat he kept sopping up off his forehead. "Not everyone can compete, ya hear? Only the finest among ye have a shot at this here prize!"

His doting assistant, the blonde bimbo Carol with big ole boobs and wayyyy too much make-up clicked out on stage in her teeny tiny heels. After all these years, I still hadn't figured out who she was trying to impress in this town, especially since everyone knew when you went to her house on Halloween she always screamed, "Two Pieces! Only grab Two Pieces!"

I guess she had to save her monies for her hairspray or somethin.

In her hands, she held up more cash than most in this town had ever held in their hands at one time. Five-hundred-dollars, she'd said. That money would go a long long way for our family.

The mayor swept his hand out over the crowd, crying "raise yer hands if ye want to compete! My assistants will pass by and tap your arm if you're chosen. If that's you...come on up to the stage so we can get ready!"

I raised my hand, stretching in my pitiful black trash bag and standing on my tip toes, never one to miss a shot at money. Towards the front of the dance floor I noticed little Emmy, jumping up and down under her faded unicorn bedsheet with two holes cut out that I'd most likely have to sew back in later.

God Bless America...one of the assistants chose her.

Soon their selections were final, with all manner of ghouls and ghosts and goblins and vampires, and even a werewolf or two on the stage. Basically, any of those typical Halloween monsters that we all knew about were the ones they'd picked.

Jessica and I sat back and watched as they lined them up, laughing at our funny friend Anthony who was putting on quite the show rubbing his gigantic pillow belly under his goblin costume. He looked like a busted can of biscuits up there. He'd even painted his face and arms green, with spiky little ears and gnarly teeth to match. He'd gone all out.

"Uhhhhh, Wen...wait, what are they doing?" Jessica stared at the stage with a worried look in her eyes that instantly stopped my heart.

Ole Blondie was tipping a pitcher of liquid into each of their mouths, one by one, going down the line. Little Emmy Lou was next.

"Hey!" I shouted, jumping out of my chair and running for the stage. The banjos were too loud for anyone to hear me as I screamed and pushed and shoved my way through the dancers to get up to her. "Don't drink whatever the hell that is, Emmy! Don't drink it, little bug!"

My heart thumbed and bumped in my chest so hard I thought I might have a whole heart attack and die right there on the dance floor. I shouted again as Emmy Lou peeked out from under her pitiful unicorn ghostie costume and placed her little hands on either side of blondie's pitcher and took a big ole gulp of God only knew what.

Her fellow contestants were hooping and hollering, dancing around on the stage and telling their plans for the $500 if they won it.

As I stood among the remaining dancers, I realized with horror how the punch I'd drank had made me feel. My stomach churned and burned and bubbled like those stink pits down by the river where that company dumped their waste. And I wasn't the only one, either.

Everyone around me, except for the contestants who had been ushered backstage, bent over holding their bellies and leaning on one another to try and stay standing. I didn't feel like I was gonna be sick, but I sure did feel like I needed to sit down.

"And now, dancers of Dandrum!!" the mayor had reclaimed the microphone with a menacing glee, "I give you...a Craaaaaazy Costume Contest!"

The clock on the courthouse next door struck 12. Midnight on Halloween.

From behind the curtains, Jack Bolinger crawled out on all fours, growling and snarling and raring his snout back to howl at the roof. Holy fucking shit.

Jack had transformed into a real werewolf.

One glance around the room revealed that he wasn't the only one, either. Susan from Subway had sprouted feathers all over her body, her lips comin' out from her face and turning into a flesh colored abomination of what I think was supposed to be a duck. Marley Jane cried as a banshee, ripping through those unfortunate enough to be standin' right next to her.

Hell had come to Dandrum this Halloween.

The mayor laughed into the microphone, spreading his arms wide as a conductor of the chaos as the crowd unleashed their monstrous fury upon one another. I tried again to run for the stage, to find Emmy Lou and get the hell out of this damned place, but slipped on a huge pool of blood spilling out of my old third grade teacher's neck. The principal, now a zombie, feasted on her flesh.

Jessica turned up next to me, moving with a speed she'd never had before, her real fangs bared this time and her eyes growing wide at the sight of blood all around us.

"Mmmmmm." She licked her lips. "I'm suddenly so very thirsty." I didn't look back as I kept on moving, not wanting to watch as she licked and slurped at the blood splattered all across the floor.

When I got to the stage, there she was, my little bug, but I could damn near see through her now. She was crying and reached out for me, but my arms swished straight through hers.

"Sissy, Help Me!!!" she cried, as tears started falling down my face now, too. "I'm trying little bug, I'm trying!"

God dammit all. This child deserved more than that. Me. Momma. All we ever could do was try and it wasn't ever fucking good enough! I screamed, an unknown rage unleashing from my body, all my pain, my fear, my grief, my frustration. Every memory of not having money for rootbeer floats or my feet hurting from my too-small shoes. I felt it welling up in my body like an electrical storm until all of the sudden actual lightning burst from my fingertips. It crackled to the ceiling, bringing with it a cacophonous roar of thunder that silenced the room.

Among that silence, I started to laugh. Cackle, even.

I might have started the evening dressed in a trash bag, but now it was clear I'd end it as a witch.

Dr. Marie Lestrange is a multipassionate badass that plays eight musical instruments and is deathly afraid of chickens. She's the author of the gothic historical novel *Crimson Cobblestones* and hosts a weekly indie Horror podcast called Moths to the Flame. She's obsessed with research into the macabre, true crime, and occultish practices and is also the founding chairman of the Horror Writers Association Tennessee Chapter. When not writing, she and her writer husband, Bert, love traveling with their little Hobbit outside of the East Tennessee mountains they call home. **Links:** https://linktr.ee/lestrangebooks

THE DEVIL WEARS DOCKERS

BILL FREAS

A crisp, cool autumn breeze swept through the picturesque campus of the Heart of Grace Academy, an all-girls Catholic boarding school tucked away in a pristine enclave of dense forests and rugged mountains in upstate New York. It was the day of All Hallows Eve. A solemn, uneasy shroud fell upon the campus every year on this date.

Once a decade, on Halloween, the school suffered the tragic and ominous death of a student or staff member. Today, a special prayer vigil was underway in the campus cathedral. Only thirty or so students were in attendance, including a feisty foursome of eleventh-grade friends: Kristi – the sassy leader, Violet – the good girl, Zoe –the clueless one, and Dora – Kristi's sidekick. The four knelt in a pew far in the back of the sizable yet cozy cathedral, gossiping at a whisper volume instead of praying on this somber and mysterious day.

"I'm beginning to think that this place isn't as fun as I thought it was going to be," Kristi said.

Dora chimed in, "Tell me about it. All this praying is making my knees hurt."

"And a curfew? Gimme a freakin' break." Kristi added.

"You guys better start praying, or we're gonna get nailed," Violet said.

Kristi replied, "I am praying. Praying that the boys' school moves closer."

"I thought this was going to make me a better person," Zoe said.

"Yeah, maybe if you wanna be a shriveled-up, middle-aged virgin librarian," Kristi retorted.

A stern nun in the front of the church became aware of the girls' soft chattering.

"Shh!!"

"I told you we'd get caught," Violet said.

Kristi rolled her eyes. "Get a grip, Violet. Little miss goodie two-shoes here is afraid she might tick off one of the fine police nuns patrolling the cell block."

Zoe interceded, "Maybe we should start praying."

"In your case, Zoe, I'd recommend it. In fact, go light a candle," Kristi replied.

Zoe smiled and departed for the votive candles up near the altar.

"Maybe I'll go light one, too," Kristi added.

"A candle?" Dora asked her.

"No, a cigarette."

"Not a good idea. We need to be serious here. This will look really good on our transcripts.

Let's not screw it up," Violet said.

Kristi chuckled softly. "Transcripts? Ha, please. Keep your straight As. I'll take the two Bs: boys and beer."

Farther ahead in the pews, another student seemed to be suffering from a very strange coughing spell. Helena, a quiet loner of the same age, was the source of the odd hacking, and she appeared quite restless in her seat.

"Oh, boy. Freakshow's at it again," Kristi commented.

"What is wrong with her?" Dora inquired.

"A mystery that has plagued us since we were good, little acolytes."

The nun was once again agitated by the murmuring.

"Shh! Ladies, please. This is a vigil of silent reflection."

Helena peered around the church bizarrely while scratching her skin, as if she was covered in fire ants.

"Look at her. Helena is a total nutjob," Kristi said.

Helena abruptly sat still and turned around slowly in her seat to face the three gossiping girls several pews behind her. Her expression was cold and grim. A voice to the girls' right side snapped their attention away from their peculiar classmate.

"Are you young ladies using this time as an opportunity to cultivate your spirits, in holiness?"

The three girls looked to their right and observed Father Matteon, a confident and respected residing priest, standing near them at the end of the pew.

Violet answered, "Yes, Father."

"Yes, Father," Dora followed.

"Good. Strong prayer will bring you redemption. Continue your Rosary, girls," the priest said.

"Yes, Father," Violet replied.

The priest strolled ahead, passing Helena on his way. Her offsetting appearance and weird behavior struck him noticeably oddly, but he continued on without addressing it.

The day moved along, and the sun eventually faded behind the mountains before the shadows of Halloween night took their rightful place among the young inhabitants of the campus. The foursome of friends threw on their pajamas and settled into their candlelit dorm room. Kristi retrieved the group's trusty bottle of cinnamon schnapps, taking a big swig and then passing it along to the other girls.

"Now, this is what I call a day's-end devotion," Dora said.

"I am fully devoted to finishing this bottle," Kristi added.

Zoe spoke up, "Save me some, Dora."

"There's plenty. Remember, Violet won't drink any. She's a delicate and devout Catholic flower," Dora replied.

"And tomorrow morning, you all will be wilting Catholic flowers with major hangovers. Good luck explaining that to Father Matteon," Violet retorted.

"Oh, lighten up, Mother Theresa," Kristi said to her. Suddenly, there was a pounding on the door.

Kristi perked up nervously. "Oh, crap! Nun patrol! Put it under the bed!"

"Whose bed?" Dora asked.

"I don't know! It doesn't matter!"

"Mints! We need mints!" Zoe exclaimed.

Zoe rummaged through her bag, for breath mints, as the pounding occurred at the door again.

"Uh, just one minute! We'll be right there, Sister!" Kristi called out, buying time.

Zoe retrieved the mints, and the girls threw some into their mouths. Swiftly, they composed themselves and prepared for the impending inspection. Kristi then marched over to the door and opened it, only to find no one there. She poked her head out into the hall. Not a single being was anywhere in sight.

"Well, that's funky."

"Who was it?" Zoe asked.

"Probably Gina and the other skanks, with a lame attempt at a Halloween scare prank."

She closed the door, and to their surprise, the pounding instantly went off yet again.

"What the hell?!"

Kristi yanked open the door once more to find nothing.

"Okay, this is getting old."

Violet spoke up, "Maybe it's not a joke. Maybe it's a sign."

"A sign?" Dora asked.

"From you-know-who," Violet answered.

Kristi scoffed, "Oh, stop, please."

"What person could knock on our door and be able to get away that fast, Kristi? It's not possible," Violet said. With no answer, Kristi simply sent her a frustrated glance.

"Think about it," Violet added.

Zoe was quickly growing anxious. "You guys, I'm getting really freaked out."

Their conversation was interrupted by the intermittent sound of small stones lightly smacking the outside of the room's main window.

"What is that?" Zoe asked. The edgy girls hurried over to the window and peered down at the courtyard outside their dorm, where a dark, shadowy figure jetted around in an abnormal and inhuman fashion. This ghostly figure below them almost resembled their peculiar classmate, Helena. Although, it moved far too fast and erratically to confirm that.

"What the hell are we watching?" Dora asked.

"I don't know," Kristi replied.

"Kind of looks like Helena," Violet added.

Shockingly, the door, left open by Kristi moments ago, slammed closed by itself with force. The startled girls screamed and whipped around toward the door, staring at it, frozen and terrified.

"Let's get our asses to bed. Now!" Kristi said.

The four friends raced into their respective beds and hid under the covers. Before long, they dozed off to sleep, soon entering a dream state they wish they never had experienced. Each girl floated through a dark nocturnal fog that led her to the surface of a creepy lake long forgotten in an abandoned state park deep in a vast forest up at the New York-Canada border. Each girl was slowly pulled beneath the surface into the murky waters, drifting deeper and deeper into the uncertain, unnerving aquatic environment. The desolate darkness soon broke as a menacing glow of supernatural origin, greenish gold in color, appeared and illuminated the grim, frightening silhouette of what looked like an otherworldly creature, a demonic entity perhaps.

It raised its inhuman arms and let out a sinister growl that seemed to make the uncanny glow around it stronger. Soon, a force gently pulled each girl in closer toward the figure, and the macabre glow began strobing. The conclusion of this terrible confrontation was uncertain because none of the four friends ever spoke of their nightmare, a nightmare they unknowingly shared. Its residue lingered and was palpable upon waking– a presence they couldn't shake.

Morning finally broke, and a fresh day was ushered in by some early sunshine, attempting to dissolve the chilling atmosphere that veiled the school yesterday and on every Halloween each year. The foursome of friends sat in theology class, weary and still disturbed by the haunting events of last night, while Father Matteon taught his daily lesson. The nun from the prayer vigil sat next to the priest's desk, assisting him with paperwork and other classroom duties.

"It's important that we understand the sacraments and the role they play in our daily faith," the priest lectured. "The beast himself, along with his hellish disciples, will challenge your hearts and souls and test your very beliefs in the Holy Trinity."

Several seats down from the four friends, the strange girl, Helena, struggled while taking in the religious lecture. Every time the priest mentioned a holy name, she writhed in torment.

"But do not ever take the power of the Lord God, for granted. For He shall have the last say over the wicked and evil of heart," he spoke.

Helena's behavior did not go unnoticed by the four friends, who stared at her silently and with great concern. Helena's unsettling motions were soon accompanied by a soft, foreboding chanting that poured out of her mouth insistently.

"And the beast will be defied and will lose its malicious grip on the good of heart before it is cast back down into the bowels of Hell, where it belongs!" the priest declared.

The friends were met with a terrifying sight when Helena turned to look at them. Her face was pale and scarred, and her eyes were rolled over white. The nun sensed something amiss and scanned the room, with her eyes, expecting to validate her keen awareness.

"There is a pall over this school, a threatening cloud. It comes once a year.

Yesterday was its homecoming. Its roots lie deep in the earth here, in the soil and nature on and around our campus. Its origins are ancient, but our faith is constantly new and fresh, which will always render us the victors over its wicked powers and malevolent influence," the priest said.

Zoe screamed, which seized the attention of the entire classroom. Helena sprung up from her chair and bellowed a cryptic phrase loudly in Sumerian, her voice gravelly and demonic. The nun cried out in shock as Helena went ballistic, attacking her classmates violently. Then, the girl stormed over to Father Matteon, wrapped her hands around his throat, and choked him with an unnatural strength and the full intent to kill.

With the assistance of several other girls, the nun wrestled Helena off the priest. The man of the cloth swiftly gathered himself and boldly recited a special Latin prayer while spritzing the possessed student, with holy water from a small bottle he retrieved from his pocket. Within mere moments, Helena calmed and appeared to return to normal again. The frightened, traumatized girl wept in the arms of the consoling nun while the four friends clutched one another and gripped their rosary beads tightly.

Father Matteon caught his breath and wiped the sweat from his brow before finally addressing the shocking incident. "Evil appears in many forms, my children. This Halloween, it decided to come in person."

Studying under esteemed writers Sonny Sykes and Charles McClelland, Bill
Freas continued his education at West Chester University before he was hired
in 2002 as the head writer of a TBS sketch-comedy pilot that ultimately did not
make it to series. Subsequently, he optioned or sold over two dozen scripts, which
included shorts, features, and pilots. As an author, he has written more than twenty
published short stories, including three full collections. His produced credits as a
writer span multiple genres and mediums. Currently, Bill also heads up Oceanicom
Films' development department, where he oversees the development of US and
international film and TV projects for the Australian company. Along with script,
development, and production consultation, Bill is also a staff writer for Vancouver
production company Foresight Entertainment, with which he has had an active
partnership for over fifteen years.

EVEN IN DEATH

ANDY HOLBERRY

July 17th

The sun shone brightly through the leaves and limbs of the tall oaks on Brazos Street.

People, clad in shorts and thin t-shirts, pushed mowers through the long grass they had allowed to spring up over time. The electric motors humming quietly while the bigger, petrol driven models growled up and down the street. Others, the more sensible among them, sat in the shade, sipping ice-cold lemonade, and watched as some friendly neighborhood girl or boy, desperate to earn some summer money, did the work for them.

The home owners would be happy to shell out the ten or twenty bucks to have it done for them. It was a lot less than they would have to pay for a professional gardening service. Young children splashed about in inflatable pools full of rapidly cooling water, their parents and guardians having to top it up with fresh, colder water ever so often.

Everything was a scene of calm and happy coexistence.

The houses were almost identical in size and shape, homes added to with flares of creativeness and individual taste. A lawn full of gnomes here, some porches hung with brightly coloured flowers in baskets, swinging gently in the breeze that blew through fretfully.

All told, a good place to live...safe.

Todd Green strolled down the street, his school bag swinging easily on his shoulders.

Today was a good day. Nor only had he aced the pop quiz, but Emma Stone had sat next to him at lunch. She had worn that small pleated skirt and their legs had touched briefly. He was sure she had smiled; that little side smile that all the other bits loved. When she wasn't looking he had leant in and taken a sniff of her hair...she smelled amazing. As he left school, the smile on his face had been locked into place.

He walked down the street still thinking of her shapely legs, his senses still picking up that lingering scent.

He didn't realize that he walked off the sidewalk and into the street.

The car, a big v8 muscle car, cherry red, barreled down the middle of the road, its engine howling. The driver had been drinking for most of the morning, celebrating a big win on the horses, more than a few drinks filling his stomach. He dropped the cigarette he had been smoking and it fell to the floor. He took his eyes off the road for ten seconds...just a short time in the greater scheme of things...but it was long enough.

The front of the vehicle slammed into the side of Todd's legs instantly breaking both of them. He was thrown onto the bonnet and then flipped over the top. He landed awkwardly and his arm folded underneath him, the rough texture of the asphalt tearing open his shirt and his flesh from shoulder to wrist. The bones in his upper arm shattered, splinters flying in all directions. His head bounced off the corner of the pavement and caved in on the side, his eye popping like a grape in the orbit. Several teeth were knocked from his jaw and he bit a chunk from his tongue.

He rolled once, twice...coming to rest against the base of a freshly trimmed hedge.

The car had come to a halt, its engine ticking, the man thinking what to do. Self preservation won out and deciding, he put his foot to the floor and sped away.

The man who owned the house called the police and an ambulance, but when they arrived; lights and sirens blaring, Todd was beyond caring.

October 31st

Eyes opened and all he could see was darkness.

He tried to move but his body was taking a while to command, to come to terms with its new state of being. Everything felt numb as if he had the worst case of pins and needles ever.

He took a deep breath trying to center himself.

A minute passed...two, then five. He realized he still had not exhaled.

Reaching up, as much as he could in the space he had, he placed a hand on his chest. The ribs did not expand or contract, the heart within was not beating, the lungs flat, no longer drawing air.

Something was seriously wrong.

He felt something close over his body and felt along its length; wooden with cushioning of some kind.

Using both hands now he pushed against the solid barrier that trapped him, placing the flat of his palms and pushing with all his strength.

It moved, lifting an inch, then two. Soon he could get a hand in the gap and whatever it had been slid to one side, tilting and crashing to the floor.

With an effort he sat up, the darkness not as absolute as it had been as his eyes adjusted.

He was in some sort of room, tall and made of stone. In front of him was a barred gate.

He was in a tomb– a crypt.

The truth hit him like a lightning bolt and he remembered it all, the memories flooding his atrophied brain. The accident, the pain...the deep dark fall into nothing.

Todd Green gave a yell of denial and anguish as he lay in his coffin.

He didn't know how long he had been there but he had to move...there was something he had to do, somewhere he had to go.

Someone to kill.

The thought entered his head as quick as that. Yes, he had someone to kill and he knew who. He remembered the car, and knew he had seen it before. It was usually parked close, the driver well known to the neighborhood.

He got out of the casket, standing unsteadily on legs that had been reset after the breaks. He could not stand fully upright, his spine would not obey his instructions to straighten as it once had. Turning, he saw the stone lid of the tomb had been previously moved or else he would never have been able to escape. Someone had made sure he would be mobile tonight. He shuffled to the gate and lifted a hand, hoping that it would be unlocked. The iron gate swung open with a squeal, the sound echoing into the still of the night.

Todd stepped out into the graveyard where he had lain since his death.

Gravestones stood in rows like sentinels in the ankle-deep fog. Mounds of disturbed earth lay all around as if something, a great many somethings, had crawled out from the damp earth. Statues of angels keeping silent vigil. There was nobody else, either the living or the dead, visible.

He was alone.

Why he was up once more in the land of the living and not still slumbering with the rest of the dead, he did not know...not yet.

He shuffled down the long central path towards the front of the boneyard.

As he approached the large ornate gates he saw they stood open. One swung on a single shattered hinge, the other laying flat on the floor. Beyond the gates he could hear the first shouts and cries, low screams and maniacal laughter. The pleading of those still alive, and the low moans of the dead.

Todd went through the gap that had once been the gates and out into the street.

Figures moved through the fog.

There looked to be two groups; those who ran...the ones who screamed and cried, and those who followed in their wake. These brought down the first group with grasping hands and tearing teeth. There were fights everywhere he looked. Figures in costume; vampires, ghosts and witches... creatures from myth and movie screen tackling real monsters.

At first Todd was shocked but that faded as he realized something had changed within him.

A feeling surfaced, slamming home like a sledge hammer blow.

He was very, very hungry.

A figure ran at him, a man, skidding to a halt just before he hit. They fell on the floor and looked up with wide staring eyes. He wore a cape, his hair slicked back...the false fangs he wore falling from his mouth to the ground. Todd took a step and his shoe came down grinding the plastic teeth to so many pieces, he reached forwards intending to help. He opened his mouth to speak, to say everything was going to be alright, but all that emerged was a low moan. The figure scrambled back more.

They were caught by a dead man who fell on them...his rotten, splintered teeth clamping onto the man's throat. Red blood, amazingly bright, spurted like a fountain into the air, splashing against Todd's face, some of it rolling down his cheek to his lips. He was hit with a euphoric surge. His eyes saw nothing but food. He fell on the man with the other figure tearing into the stranger with utter abandon.

Todd steadily chewed on the hand and forearm that he held as he walked down the street.

Carved pumpkins sat in porches or lay shattered on paths. A few still burned with candles, blazing light from carved eyes and fanged mouths.

There was something that he had to do, somewhere he was meaning to go, but the details were blurry now, the need falling away like leaves in a high wind.

His feet carried him forward. Around him were others like him. He didn't know when they had become a group, it had happened gradually. Fires burned behind him, some of the others falling as they got too close to the flames.

Some had entered houses as they had seen people inside...the need for food, to fill that gnawing hunger inside overriding the need for self preservation.

Todd ate what he had and it helped. His thoughts were very much his own still. But details slipped with every passing second. He knew who he was, what he was, but the where he was going...what he had wanted to do when he got there was just a blur in the back of his rapidly deteriorating mind.

He didn't know how long he walked. When he got the chance to eat; whether it was bringing some fleeing person down, or picking up leftovers, he didn't care.

His mind skipped now; memories coming and going. Some he could retain with effort. Others surfaced on the screen of his mind bringing a host of emotions, then shattered apart and fell away never to be seen again.

Something whizzed past his head, the sound like a yellowjacket close to his ear, hitting a body behind him. It fell with a thud to the ground. He turned in the direction of the noise. His eyes were not working like they should. The ducts were dry, no moisture on the orbs and everything had a blurry quality to it. He detected movement but made little sense of it. Another bang and whizz, something plucked at the sleeve of his shirt. Whatever it was ricocheted off the sidewalk and flew speeding off into the night.

"Ahh...shit!"

The voice, closer now, panicked.

There was more noise, a rattle of metal but no more bangs.

The group that he was with moved towards it. They mounted steps and walked through a low fence, a couple of their number falling to impale themselves on the broad points. The other carried on regardless.

They reached a barrier and for a moment could go no further, but the press of bodies, both in front and behind, soon fixed the problem. The door to the house fell inwards and the group swarmed inside. There, smaller bangs, but just a few before the meals were brought to the ground.

Todd pushed forwards with some of the others, caught in the momentum, unable to stop himself even if he wanted to. One of his feet came down on a small plastic container and it smashed flat before cracking apart. Small wrapped things fell from its insides and rolled or were trodden underfoot. The legend 'candy bucket' was visible for a second before that, too, was gone.

He saw over the shoulders of those in front a large adult holding something that issued a thin stream of smoke in his hand. His other held a metal object that glinted in the weak light.

The first object (a gun?...where had that thought come from?) made a loud noise and one of the group to his right toppled, dragged down and under as others took his place. Cold blood hit the side of his face. Something akin to the feeling of porridge landing on a shoulder.

The hand moved, pointed at him. Another noise but softer this time. No flame issued from its end.

Todd reached forwards with the others, fingers questing, nails catching and tearing. Another noise issued as the man was dragged into the group, the bar he held doing little to save him.

Behind him were several more huddled shapes. They were different from the first; two of them had masks hanging around their necks.

Todd reached out and grabbed the closest, bringing them to his waiting jaws.

He found himself outside once again, the passage of time between incidents a blur of forgotten memories.

He was sinking deeper and deeper into pure instinct.

He had tried to keep hold of his name, of a small piece of himself in order to retain a fraction of his humanity, but even that was slipping away.

Two spots of light appeared around a turn in front of the group, headed their way. A growl like the shout of an animal accompanying them.

The thing got closer, resolving itself into a brightly coloured car, the engine roaring as it sped towards them. Whoever was behind the wheel had spotted them and had mounted the pavement, still going fast but more careful in their driving now. Still, as it shot past it caught the outside edge of the large group, throwing bodies into the air, dragging a couple underneath the wheels. The vehicle bumped over them as they got pulled under, the bodies chewed up and spat out the back...rear tyres leaving scorching black marks on the remains.

It gave a violent lurch, tried to correct. It hit the side of a building and started to slide, sparks flying from the doors as the metal scraped along brickwork.

It sped past, the driver visible for a moment, his face in sharp detail compared to the rest of the world.

Something fired inside his brain; an image of a car (the same car?) as it connected with his body.

His head followed the path of the car as it rebounded back into the road, streaks of red following it as it pulled further away. There were lumps in the red and some of his companions dropped to the floor to feed, stuffing their mouths with dripping red chunks of flesh.

Todd, or the thing that he had now become, saw the car hit the corner of another parked car and start to lift. The driver tried to correct...went too far. The car flipped onto its side and then, with a rending screech of tortured metal, landed on its roof. It dug a furrow in the asphalt and plowed into the front of a shop window, glass exploding in every direction.

He took a step in the direction of the crash.

Others had seen the impact and started in the same direction. They all moved with a singular purpose. Todd saw the man crawl from the smashed driver's side window and stagger to the back of the car. He bent down and wrenched open the back door, first pulling a bag from inside, then going back in. He pulled a limp body from the rear seat and sat there holding them to him.

Whoever it was didn't move, didn't cry out in pain. Their arms hung limply at their sides.

The man noticed the lack of movement...also the group making its way towards him. He laid the small form on the ground and stood up. He pulled something from his waist and pointed it at the group.

Two bangs, three....four.

A figure spun as it was hit in the shoulder but righted itself and staggered on. Another fell to the ground, the back of its skull a raw, ragged hole. Todd stepped into the gap that he left.

The man saw him and his arm dropped, what he held now pointing at the ground.

His mouth opened, his face wearing a look of surprise.

"No...no, it can't be," he croaked. "You're dead."

He fired twice more, the bullets hitting Todd in the side and the arm before the weapon clicked on an empty chamber. He threw it and, grabbing the bag, turned and ran into the store.

Todd followed, a line of blood leaking from the hole in his side and arm. He didn't feel the wounds, but he felt something. A feeling that was surfacing in him that he hadn't felt for a long time.

He had hate in him for the man, but didn't know why, the memory of the accident was already gone.

He walked closer to the wreck, ignoring the body, or what was left of it, on the floor, and stepped through the broken window. He stepped over the things that lay in his way; costumes in bags, plastic pitchforks and cauldrons. His head and shoulders brushed against several large black-haired spiders that hung from the ceiling. Hearing the sound of footsteps further inside the store he followed.

Stairs were becoming a problem.

The flight that the man had fled up was strewn with debris and he had a hard time navigating them. He fell several times, the last fall breaking his nose and caving in a cheek on a piece of masonry.

He made it to the top and stood in the long hallway there, unsure of what to do next. If the man had not made a noise, he would have never known where to go next.

A door closed gently to his right and he went in that direction, stopping when he reached it. With the last of his freewill he turned and walked into it. The door wouldn't open even though there was no handle...no lock, and he heard a grunt on the other side as something pushed back.

"Please, please go away. Leave me alone."

The voice that came from the other side was pleading, close to breaking, but Todd didn't know that. All he was aware of was the presence of food; of warm blood inside the room.

He pushed harder.

He knew he had to get to the man, had to...to what? He couldn't remember why.

He stepped back now and then fell against the door. It gave an inch then slammed back into its frame.

"Please...," the voice begged.

Drool fell from Todd's lips...he pushed gain, the door moving once more. Again it slammed shut but not before he had seen an image of the man inside the room in a large mirror. He also saw himself– but the image was of a stranger so he ignored it.

Again he pushed, moving his feet as he did so. One of them stayed partly in the room as the door started to close.

"No, no...no!"

The cry was more a shout now, a moan of denial...of impending doom. Todd got one hand inside, gripped the edge of the door, then the other. The barrier inched open.

The man on the other side backed up, lifted a pipe above his head as he went. It should have been all over, there was only him and Todd. All he had was a burning need to avenge himself (where had that thought come from?) and his teeth and hands.

The man fell over the bag where he had dropped it. He fell and hit his head, the makeshift weapon falling from his suddenly nerveless fingers. Todd walked towards him.

The figure held up his hands trying to defend himself from the attack he knew was coming. His eyes ticked to the bag and in desperation he held it in front of him, using it as a barrier.

Todd tore it away, throwing it to one side. It hit the wall spilling cash and food from inside and dug his fingers, as rigid as steel rods, into the man's chest. He pushed and his nails sank deeper touching something that pulsed and shuddered.

The man looked up at him with eyes wide with shock.

"I'm sorry....so....so sorry. I didn't see you. Didn't...didn't see you."

The dead boy walked down the road. The group he was with had grown as they hunted through neighborhoods, clearing streets and houses as they went.

Blood dried around his mouth and chin, drying to a crust on his shirt. His hands were covered in gore and he occasionally lifted them to his lips to suck at the bits of flesh that sat there.

All memory of who he once was had gone.

All that remained was the wails of the living, and the moans of the dead.

My name is Andy Holberry.

I herald from an
island that no-one has heard of just
south of one of the busiest shipping
lanes in the world.

I love to write and read...a lot.

Favourite authors are Guy Smith,
James Herbert and Stephen King. If
some people are to be believed, I am
part robot, and I'm good with that lol

DARK OUT

Jacob Pittman and Cody Nukem

October 3oth - 1990 - 11:59 pm

Carved pumpkins decorated the porches of the quiet neighborhood. Fog covered the damp pavement as the teenagers traveled through the dark night. Mike led his four friends through a hole in the fence. The abandoned school towered above them the closer they got. The quiet town was sound asleep as time crossed into Devil's Night.

"Why are we doing this?" Amy asked nervously, rubbing her cold arms.

"I told you we have to see the crime scene before they tear down the building," Mike said with irritation.

Frank walked behind the others, cautiously looking over his shoulder to check for lurking shadows following them. "I don't know how good of an idea this is."

"Don't be a pussy. I told you I'll kill you myself if you try to back out," Mike threatened.

Chelsea sighed when the group arrived at the boarded window. "What if the cops catch us? We can get into big trouble for going in there."

Mike released his grip on the wooden plank and directed his attention at the blonde-haired girl who dared interrupt his plan. He walked to her, his toxic energy forcing her to back her body against the bricks. "We are doing this! End of discussion."

"Why do you want to see where kids were slaughtered, man? It's messed up, don't you think?" Doug chimed in.

"Listen, back in 84, Horace Pyke killed over twenty people inside these walls. That is the only interesting thing to ever happen in this wasteland of a town. I want to see the real deal before it's too late. Man up and let's go."

Mike ripped the boards out and created an opening. He climbed in first, his leather jacket catching a nail and ripping as he fell to the filthy floor. "Alright, get in here, Amy." He reached for her small hand and helped her through and continued until the group was all inside.

Frank and Doug carried the flashlights, spreading a soft glow through the dimly lit interior. The only other light came from the full moon that hung low over the sleepy town.

"Okay, we are in. Now what?" Chelsea asked, shivering in her shoes both from the weather and the horrible feeling that twisted her stomach. The idea of getting caught terrified her but, also being in the building that had such a plagued reputation.

Mike smiled with a sinister grin as they began to explore. All the articles and research he did on Horace Pyke flashed before his eyes. The murderer had become a hero to him. A man who stood against the system and took a lethal stand and hacked his classmates and teachers to pieces. He cut off limbs, carved off flesh, and decapitated a popular girl who rejected him. Mike got lost in the sea of blood that flooded his thoughts. He wanted to be like Horace. He wanted to show the world he was worthy of carrying on the legacy.

1984

Horace Pyke felt a cold chill crawl up his back like a whisper of terror upon his nerves. Standing in the hall, alone, he looked at his wristwatch and saw that the time was 3 pm. How in the hell was it already three?

It was around 12:30 when he stepped out of the lunch room and started heading for his next class. He could remember as far as pushing the doors open and stepping through, and then, it happened to him as fast as blinking. He was now standing in front of the school entrance. Had been for a while. His legs were sore, the can of cola in his right hand was room temperature. He had just bought it before leaving the cafeteria. The doors were locked now. He dropped his school bag and the soda and tried to pry them open. No good. He walked around to the back exit of the building and pushed it, but it didn't budge. He was getting scared now. He ran to every fire exit and they too would not open.

He was trapped. How?

With his back against the last fire exit, he slid down sitting on the marble floor. He looked at his watch again. It was now 7 pm. He gasped. First, he lost three hours. Now, another four! "This thing is broken." He goes to a window in math class and tried to pry the window open in vain. Then, he realized that it was already almost dark out. He stepped backward, confused, and frightened. He sat down in the teacher's chair. It really was past 7 pm. He lost 7 hours!

What in the world was going on.

None of the telephones had dial tones. Not even the payphone close to the entrance. Nothing. "oh no..." he said, putting the phone back on the hook. And he turned to walk back down the hall and head for the principal's office; Principal Sully had his own line right on his desk. Everyone who went to Gateway High School knew about it. Sully was a mean bastard alright. Often, when you were sent to the Principal's office, he'd make you stand up for sometimes hours while he chatted away. Horace was very young when he first was sent to his office, because one kid lied to the teacher saying that he was whispering curse words into her ear. Which wasn't true, because Horace didn't swear. He was as well-behaved a kid as you hope for. His parents were the Christian conservative types. And though they were strict, they raised him to be a gentle and kind person. And that's who he was. He didn't know why he was sent to the principal's office at first. He stood there for maybe 30 minutes, which felt hours to the young mind, before Principal Sully stood he hung up the phone, then he grabbed a flat wood paddle off of the wall with holes drilled into it and moved towards Horace, fear coursing through him.

Horace's imagination ran wild as Sully stood behind him and lined up to swing the paddle. He shook bracing for the pain but when the impact came he didn't feel anything. Instead, everything went black. When the colors returned he was back in class. He felt as if he had been dreaming and suddenly woke from a nightmare, but he was in a different classroom and it was almost time to go home.

The blackouts didn't return until today and what he experienced with Sully was different. He lost time, but now he had lost his full day. He was terrified to think his body was operating without him. Horace leaned against the principal's wall and lowered, sinking his face into his knees.

Make them bleed...

Make them suffer...

Make them burn with me!

A voice spoke to him from the shadows. Horace panicked, hurrying to his feet to abandon the office, when he made it outside the door everything went black again.

When he woke his hands were covered with a dried scarlet color. Inside his tight grip was a knife. He had no memory of it. It was gray and black with a design engraved on the blade. He didn't know what it was. His guts felt like they may rupture when he spotted the dangling flesh hanging from the serrated teeth of the weapon. Slowly he looked around to see all the corpses of his classmates. Everyone was dead.

1990

"We should split up," Mike insisted.

Frank argued, "Why would we do that?"

Mike turned to him. "It's a big place, and we don't know which room it happened in. You take Chelsea and Doug and look around here, Amy and I will go upstairs."

"Sounds good to me," Doug chimed in, handing his flashlight over. The groups went their separate ways.

"Why the hell did you agree to this?" Frank started.

Doug kept his eyes on the floor. "That guy gives me the creeps. What the hell are we doing with him? He's trouble, man.

"Don't blame me, the girls like him."

"I thought he was cute! I never said we should follow him to a murder scene!" Chelsea quickly added.

Mike rammed his shoulder into the door of the old science class, forcing his way into the room. He scanned the room and thought maybe it was it, but another wrong room. It ground his nerves that he never got to attend school in the building where Horace Pyke unleashed his wrath. After the horrible event, the town closed the school for good. Nobody wanted to step foot on the bloodstained tiles ever again. So much death lingered in the air.

"Why do you think he did it?" Amy asked. She hated being in the building but didn't mind being alone with Mike. He was kind of a jerk, but she was attracted to him regardless. A piece of her liked the way he ordered the others around. "My guess, he got sick of dealing with people. It happens all the time. A person can only take so much of society's ilk before they lose their shit and ape out." Mike said.

"Ape out?"

"You know. Human nature. Civilized society has only ever suppressed our basic instincts. We are just animals too. And sometimes, young men like Horace come along to remind us of that fact." Mike delighted in this notion as he fumbled with some of the science equipment still left behind. "Yeah but, it's still wrong..." Amy said with unease, starting to notice Mike's unsettling enthusiasm. She took a careful step back towards the door.

"Amy...I am disappointed in your lack of a nuanced perspective. Society is always changing its mind about what's right and wrong, or what minority group deserves to be coddled while leaving others in the gutters."

She had turned to reach for the door handle. She looked back, Mike was gone from sight. Just the dark cold emptiness of the lab, slowly becoming possessed with a presence of terror hiding in each shadow and around the corners of each work desk, peaking out at her in her mind's eye, the line between reality and imagination merging until she could almost see the ghoulish faces smiling as they retreat to the shadows back around the desks. "Killing a room full of assholes is wrong…"

The door handle finally turned and she pulled it open, just for a force to slam it back shut. She saw Mike's hand on the door, her eyes following the arm to his shoulder, and then she saw into his eyes.

Cold, blank, evil. Then he said, "Was it really wrong?"

Frank stepped out of the English class pulling the door shut behind him. "You figured that nut job would have at least read up enough to know which classroom it was. I can't stay here all goddamn night."

"Like you have anything else going on besides sitting at home jackin' it." Doug said. "You're only here because you're scared of the nut job too."

Frank retorted. "I can't believe I let Amy talk me into coming here. She just wanted to get closer to Mike," Chelsea said.

"Is she into the bad boy types or something?" Doug questioned.

"More like the psycho types," Frank added.

A scream echoed down the halls. "That sounded like Amy!" Chelsea said.

"Amy! Mike!…Shit." Frank said. "Where the hell are they? Damn it, I knew this was a bad idea to come here!"

Chelsea looked through the little window on the science class door. "Hey! Look at this." She pushed it open, the boys following behind her. She bent down to one knee, and there, on the floor was a pool of darkness. She clicked her flashlight on, and it shined from the reflective surface of the wet blood.

"What the hell man…" Doug said over Chelsea's shoulder. "What the hell happened to them?"

Frank raised his hand to his neck, "It was that nut job! Goddamn it, why did I let her go off alone with that freak."

"You don't know if he did this Frank. What if something happened to him too?" Chelsea reasoned. "Either way, we need to get the fuck out of here and call the cops," Frank spit back, pacing the room. He turned for the door but stopped dead in his tracks. Frozen. "Jesus Christ..." he said, backing away. The other two turned around. Shock and horror came over them just the same, as they all recognized the disemboweled corpse hanging up next to the exit. When the door opens, it would conceal the body, but not when you were on your way out. "It's...It's Amy..." Her entrails dangled as low to the ground from an opening in her abdomen. Her face contorted in a look of agony, her mouth agape, her eyes unmoving, lifeless.

Frank bolted for the door first with the other two following with the same terrified momentum. The three made it back to the school entrance. Smashing into the doors that now refused to open. "What the Hell! The doors, they're all chained up!" Chelsea said. Frank violently shook the chains. "Fuck! Where is the window we came in at?!"

"I don't know! This place is a fucking maze. Let's try breaking through another one!" Doug spit, rushing to a new room to the side of the doors. All hope was gone when the kids spotted the bars on the opposite side of the glass. They were trapped.

They ran back into the hall when a static shock pierced through their ears. The intercom came to life with a faint raspy voice spilling through the speakers.

Make them bleed...
Make them suffer...
Make them burn with me!
Make them bleed...
Make them suffer...
Make them burn with me!

Bring them to me... Bring them to me... Bring them to ME!!!

The voice tore through the school. The kids ran as fast as they could when they came to a dead stop at the stairs. Standing at the top was Mike, covered head to toe in blood. He began to descend his boots smacking hard against the steps and making a popping echo like a gun being fired. The kids stood almost paralyzed watching him get closer. Halfway down Mike suddenly stumbled and came barreling down the remainder of the way. He clutched his abdomen and wheezed for air.

"Help... He cried out."

Frank stretched his arm to block his friends from approaching the pleas. "It's a trap."

"Please..." Mike continued to beg, breathing heavier now.

"I think he's hurt badly," Chelsea said.

Against his better judgment, Frank moved closer to examine the situation. Chelsea left Doug's side and followed behind her friend.

Mike's head dropped to the floor, leaving him to stare lifelessly at the ceiling. Frank saw a huge wound oozing blood from Mike's stomach.

Chelsea covered her mouth and backed into the lockers that ran along the wall. "Who did this to him?" She whimpered.

"I don't... I don't know..." Frank checked his pulse and confirmed what everyone feared. Another member of their group was dead.

"This can't be happening. This can't be fucking real!" Chelsea grasped chunks of her hair sickened by the truth before her. Frank came to her and wrapped her tight in a hug. "It's okay. We will get out of here. We won't let anything happen to you, right, Doug?"

"Doug," Frank asked again, unconfident in the silence.

They turned and jumped back.

Behind Doug stood a shadowy figure. Doug's mouth was smothered by the stranger's hand. The man used his free hand to lodge his knife inside of Doug's ear, killing him instantly.

"No!" Chelsea screamed as their friend's corpse dropped to the ground.

"Run! Frank demanded, grabbing Chelsea's hand and pulling her along.

Running for their lives, Frank looked through every door trying to find the window they entered. The second to last door he saw the moonlight pour through the opening Mike created. He looked behind them to see the shadowy figure approaching; walking fast with his gleaming knife in hand.

"Hurry! We need to get out of here." Chelsea hollered tugging at her friend. They made it to the window. Chelsea forced her body through. The hole felt smaller with her heart racing. Her sweatshirt got caught on a nail. She pulled, struggling to break free with Frank pushing her until she fell free.

Her body smashed hard against the ground. She looked up in time to see Frank coming through when he suddenly stopped before he was rapidly forced back inside the school.

She rose to her feet when the stranger's knife came slashing through the opening at her. She jumped back falling again. She looked into the black abyss of the building and saw her attacker for a split second. She knew it was impossible, but with her eyes, she saw Horace Pyke. He was still young and looked identical to the way he did in the newspapers.

He was still there. After all this time. He was still in the school. And now all of her friends were forever trapped inside the building with him.

Hello, this is Jacob Pittman. I am a writer and publisher, passionate about crafting better stories of suspense and horror. I am unorthadox in my prose and style, thus I bring a unique persepctive to the page. I have published stories in Horror Weekly, Creepypasta, I co created Blood-soaked Pages with my friend Cody Waltman which contained many of my favorite stories, and I am currently the General Overseer of Sinister Society. I live to share my writings with my co author's (my readers) as we explore the further regions of darker imaginings.

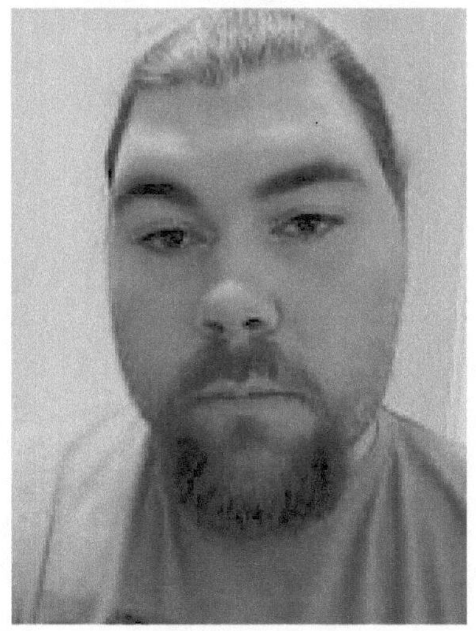

DEVIANT OFFERING

DANNA GREENWOOD

Dylan slipped out of bed quietly, leaning down to pick up his clothes off the floor. The girl lay covered with a duvet and her head turned towards the wall, unmoving. The early dawn light coming through the small window was just enough for Dylan to find where he had flung his socks and shoes the night before. After getting dressed, he crept out of the room and tiptoed down the hall.

Once outside, Dylan breathed a sigh of relief. He crossed the courtyard and headed back to his room in the fraternity house. His first class of the day was at ten, so he had plenty of time to shower and eat breakfast.

Campus was quiet at this time of the morning. The birds chirped and the air was cold and crisp. Fall leaves crunched under his feet. Dylan was excited for the party tonight. Halloween was a sacred holiday in his fraternity house. This year, he was in charge of organizing their big house party.

Dylan turned right past the physics building and stopped, the hair on his neck bristling. He looked around and saw movement by one of the bushes. There was rustling and then it stopped.

It's probably just a bird. Dylan shrugged and walked along Greek row, humming his favorite song, and thinking about the party tonight. He scanned his key card to get in the house, the door slamming behind him.

The creature with red eyes huffed a white cloud into the cold air and nestled deeper into the bushes.

The house was quiet– most guys didn't get up until noon. Someone was passed out on the couch and snoring. Dylan took the stairs two at a time up to his room.

His frat brother, Trevor, opened his door as Dylan walked by. "D-man, how was last night?"

"It was amazing, my brother," Dylan said, winking.

Trevor smiled. "Did you bone?"

"You know it." Dylan laughed.

"D-man, always the ladies man." Trevor shook his head. "You are one lucky son of a bitch."

"See you at tonight's party, man," Dylan said. "I have to get to class."

Once in his room, Dylan took the prescription bottle out of his pocket and placed it in his nightstand drawer. There was only one pill left, and he needed more.

After his classes, Dylan met up with the bros in the frat house living room to make sure everything was ready for the Halloween party.

"J-Rod, do we have all the liquor arranged?" Dylan said to the bearded guy sprawled across the couch.

"We've got six kegs of Miller Lite, and we did a Costco run for tequila, vodka, and rum," J-Rod said. "Tables are already set up for beer pong."

"Excellent," Dylan said. "And the DJ?"

"He's coming at four o'clock to set up," T-bone said, his face expressionless. His eyebrows had been shaved off during their last party.

"Great," Dylan said. "Let's meet back here around five o'clock to check in before the party starts."

As the guys were leaving, Dylan pulled J-Rod aside. "J-Rod, I need more."

"Dude, they were hard to get last time," J-Rod whispered. "I can't keep doing this for you."

Dylan handed him a hundred-dollar bill.

"Jesus," J-Rod said, stuffing the bill into his jeans. "I'll see what I can do."

"I need it by tonight, jackass," Dylan said. "There's another hundred when you give it to me."

"Okay, just chill bro," J-Rod said, walking away.

Dylan smiled to himself and then went upstairs to his room.

The creature with the red eyes stood outside the living room window, pleased with what he had seen. The Dylan boy was quite devious but was he cunning enough for Master? The creature snorted and stomped its hoof into the dirt.

Hours later, the music blasted as Dylan stumbled his way through the party. He was already six drinks deep and had chatted up several girls. Dylan felt the pills in his pocket, giving him confidence and power. He was on his way to find a girl he had just left to go to the bathroom, but the room was spinning.

There was a figure in the corner not moving. It had horns and a grotesque, mangled face and piercing red eyes – like it belonged to another world. It was Halloween, but Dylan had never seen anything so lifelike and disturbing. He staggered towards the corner to investigate, but the thing was gone when he got there.

Dylan walked in the living room to find the girl he was chatting up. She was a perfect target because the friend she had come to the party with was currently hooking up with J-Rod. Dylan grabbed a cup of beer near the keg and dropped six pills into the drink. They fizzed and dissolved quickly.

"Hey girl," Dylan said, plopping down on the couch. "I got you a drink."

"Thanks, Dylan," the girl said. "Took you long enough."

Dylan laughed, wrapping his arm around the girl's shoulders. "It'll be worth the wait, baby."

Twenty minutes later, the girl had finished the drink, and her eyes drooped. Dylan pulled her up from the couch and led her into one of the empty downstairs bedrooms.

He dropped her on the bed, getting ready to undress her, when he heard a loud snort behind him. Dylan turned and saw a towering figure – it was seven feet tall and had a man's smooth torso; one leg was human, and one leg was hairy and ended in a hoof. The creature's face was goat-like and long, with two curved horns between pointy ears. The goat man's long arms ended with giant hands and claws for fingers. Its red eyes bore into Dylan, and the thing smiled, revealing pointy, black teeth.

"What the fuck?" Dylan said, backing away from the creature.

The goat man bleated and grabbed Dylan's legs, dragging him towards the door.

Dylan came to in the forest behind the frat house. He was on the cold ground, with his head pounding. He barely heard the music of the frat party going on nearby. The goat man stood over him, his chest heaving and drool hanging out of his mouth. His red eyes glowed with anticipation.

"What were you going to do to that girl?" the creature asked, his voice gruff and raspy.

"Nothing," Dylan said, trying to get up. "I swear."

"You're not a very good liar," the goat man said. "But that's what makes you perfect."

Dylan cried. "Perfect for what?"

"The Master," the goat man said. "He tasked me with finding him someone so vile and disgusting that no one would miss him."

Dylan scrambled to his feet and the goat man kicked him down with his hoof.

"No, please," Dylan said. "What do you want with me?"

"An offering," the goat man said, grinning. "The most delicious sacrifice on Halloween night. The deviant ones are the most flavorful."

The goat man hit Dylan over the head with his clawed hand and Dylan went still. The creature picked up Dylan's legs and headed deeper in the forest, dragging Dylan behind him.

"What a delectable treat for Master's birthday." The goat man bleated and disappeared into the forest.

Danna Greenwood is an author of short stories and essays. Her horror short stories have appeared in Scare Street: Night Terrors and Blood-Soaked Pages. When she's not writing, Danna watches scary movies, reads creepy books, and goes on walks with her two furbabies. Danna lives in Huntsville, Alabama. Follow her on X: @DannaAuthor and IG: @dannaauthor.

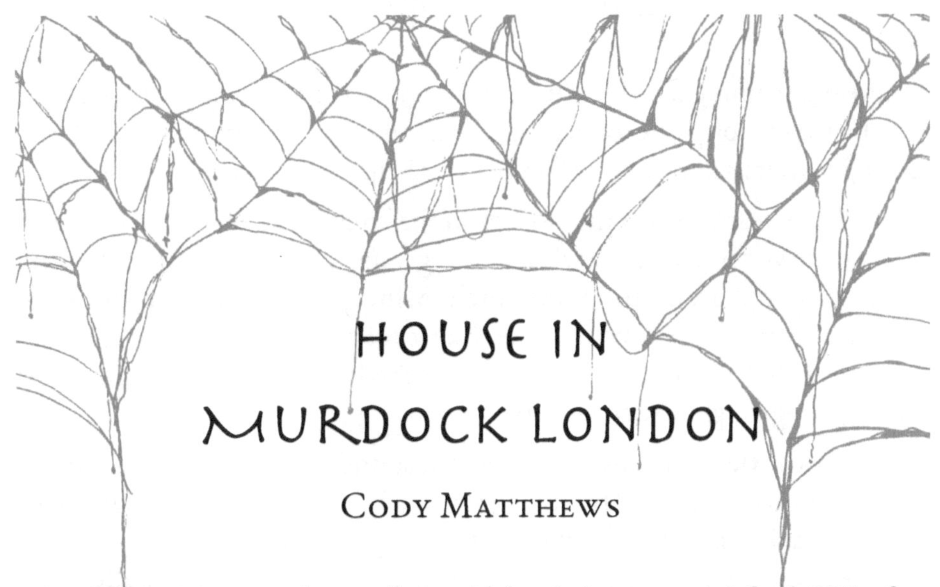

HOUSE IN MURDOCK LONDON

CODY MATTHEWS

We moved out of our old family house in Ashford, UK, after a violent break-in, something I wish I could erase from my kids' memories, but I can't. Peyton and Wesley are always going to remember their mom, Jackie, getting assaulted, and me beating an intruder with a baseball bat; but to be fair, I wasn't thinking clearly that day, mainly because I was doing everything in my power to make sure my wife and kids were safe.

I, Terrance Yate, knew there was no way we could raise our kids in the house where they watched their parents get attacked, so I found a house on the outskirts of Murdock, London. 0000 Parksfell Road. The property owner sold it to me for half the price, something I found odd considering how big it was. I took it without a second thought, thinking I was the luckiest guy on the planet to get a three-story house for the price of a one-story house.

Arriving at the house on halloween day, we all stood outside the car with our suitcases in our hands, staring at the gray and white exterior. It had a white wooden deck railing going along the front porch, and another set of white deck railing going along the top area. Then four lines of white bar-like walls going up to the roof. The wood squaring the windows was white, and the rest were gray.

I should've taken us standing there like we did as a sign— but I can't say I remember doing it. The house had a charming, lived-in feel to it. At the time unassuming...nothing threatening. Just the sort of place to get away from the trauma of past experiences. I remember going inside to unpack and shooting conversation with my family as we helped each other feel at home.

While tearing open the last box in the kitchen, I got a sense of danger, like someone was in the house with me. To get my mind off it, I decided to put the carved pumpkins on the front porch, Mine gave me the creeps for some reason... A fear of loss came over me. But it made no sense, We carved them before we moved in here, and I never felt like this before. But I never remember my pumpkin giving me such anxiety.

"Leave Me!" Quickly whispered, the sound not even sounding human, but not inhuman either. After being startled by the whisper that came from my pumpkin, I walked back in the house feeling strange.

For some reason, I truly believed that I was supposed to be the only one there, that I somehow owned the property for centuries, which made no sense because we just moved there. The feeling that something took over was pervasive.

All-consuming.

I suddenly felt a sense of familiarity that was almost too much, that I had been in this room, this house...before.

I couldn't stop myself. I skulked towards the counter, sliding a kitchen knife out of the holder. Prowling the house for the intruder, checking every room.

Nothing.

I made my way out on the front porch, and the moment I stepped a couple of feet from the house, I came to. "What the fuck?" I thought.

I scanned around to see where I was. I was still at the house, but just outside. I dropped the kitchen knife I had no recollection of grabbing.

"Terrance! What are you doing?" inquired Jackie, sprinting up to me with a shake in her hands. "What were you doing? Are you okay?"

"How do you answer something you weren't there for?" I asked myself in response. She continued to look at me with a questioning look in her eyes. Worry sounded too little of a term. There was something there, something I couldn't put my finger on.

I got back to the kitchen to see my kids staring at me like I was a deranged stranger, almost like I wasn't there, petrifying me to death. How are they staring at me like this, yet I can't even remember what I did? Thank god I saved myself by suggesting ice cream, something that my nine-year-old, Wesley, still loves, but Peyton has grown out of, or so she says. Even though Peyton is seventeen, Jackie and I still see her as our baby girl. Which is why I like to imagine that a part of her still lights up when we go to get ice cream, but instead, she asks, "Since Wesley's getting ice cream, can I get a new phone?"

I hesitated, but knew I couldn't give Wesley ice cream and Peyton nothing, so I agreed to get her a new phone afterwards.

At Rally's Ice Cream Shop, I gave Wesley a piggyback, holding onto his little legs hanging from my neck, listening to him laughing as I made strange noises, something I've done with him since he was three. Knowing he wouldn't stay this age forever, the fear I had with Peyton when she was his age. After the strange experience in the front yard, and the apparent stalking of the house with a kitchen knife, I was more scared than ever for the kids' safety. Feeling like I hadn't done or given enough for them, still not able to shake the looming fear that something was a threat.

On the way to the phone store, we all reminisced about the times at the old family house in Ashford, echoing the time when Jackie did her embarrassing hokipoki dance and actually won a talent show at our church, then the time when Peyton accidentally stepped off the stage during a ballet performance. But while Jackie has always been good about taking jokes about herself, Peyton hasn't. She got agitated, and even though it was awkward for a little bit, there was a part of me that was glad we weren't at the house.

But the trip wasn't long enough. We were back at the house, and the spinning feeling hit me as soon as we walked in the door. The upbeat, happy, and somewhat awkward mood shifted to dread and animosity. The kids went to their room. Jackie and I sat on the bed watching TV before I realized that her eyes were starting to swell. She put her face in her hands, and mumbled something that sounded like demands.

"Jackie? You okay?"

Her body jerked like she was convulsing. I thought for a minute that she was having a nervous breakdown, something she's had before, but as I attempted to grab the phone on our dresser, Jackie stood up with her back facing me,

"THIS IS MINE! NO ONE LIVES IN ME BUT ME!"

What am I supposed to say to something like that? I stood there completely still, unable to speak coherent sentences. She turned to me with swollen bug eyes, her face pressed into itself, making her cheekbones more visible. She walked towards me as if every bone in her body was broken. Bruises appeared on her body. I was crying on the inside, wanting to help her, but she wasn't the person I knew. Then:

"GET OUT!" she thundered without blinking. "I'M NOT YOUR HOME! I'M NOT YOUR PROPERTY! GET OUT! GET OUT!"

The "get outs" gradually descended into a deep, roar-like tone, except it wasn't a roar; it was a much more deranged-sounding, and something you would have to be there for to know. There was more screaming, but I don't remember what else she said. I just remember her face being caved in, and her eyes being bulgy and swollen with a grayness around her eyes, not blinking as she got closer and closer to me with her bruised body and inhuman gaze.

What the fuck was happening? I knew something was wrong with the house because this was the second time one of us zoned out or experienced bizarre changes. She eventually came out of the... trance, or whatever it was, and lay in bed. I immediately went to Peyton's room to see if everything was alright, and if they heard anything, asking Peyton three times if she heard mom screaming.

"Mom was screaming? What was she screaming about?"

I could tell by her tone and furrowed brows that she actually didn't know what I was talking about, something you would think would make me feel better, but it didn't.

"Can I get a new car?" asked Peyton, as if she had forgotten what we were talking about.

"Sure, honey."

I wandered into Wesley's room, finding him standing in the middle of the room with a swarm of red flies around his body and tiny blood spots on his face. The room looked like it was moving, red little bodies crawling on and flying past the wall. But when I got a better look at the flies, they had transparent skin, legs that looked like thin transparent tentacles, and wings that looked like transparent white skin then wings. They were the size of giant hornets.

I rushed in swatting at them, finally getting to the middle of the room, and suddenly he was on the right-hand corner. I made one more attempt to grab him, only for him to appear on the left side of the room. The flies migrated above Wesley, his eyes becoming a dark hole, swirling in a circle above him before shooting down into his eyes.

"Wesley!" I cried.

Wesley collapsed. A sobbing fit came out of me like a sickness. I couldn't stop. I felt the heavy sadness burrowed in my chest, holding Wesley's unconscious body in my arms, praying he wasn't dead.

"What the fuck? What the fuck?" I said, knowing the situation, but not knowing where the words were coming from. I felt less and less safe the more I was in the house. Carrying Wesley's unconscious body, I rushed to Peyton and Jackie.

"Get what you need, we're leaving!" I demanded, and even though I knew this wasn't gonna be easy, I pushed anyways. "Don't ask where or why! Just pack what you want you need and get in the car!"

"Why? Where are we going?" Peyton irritably responded.

I paced myself to the car, keeping my head down and eyes looking forward. Just in case someone got concerned. I tugged the car handle, feverishly pushing the unlock button on the car fob, pushing every button but the one I intended; causing the car alarm to go off. Shaking, and taking quick glances behind me, I pushed the unlock button as my vision got blurry.

"Get in the car!" I cried, finally getting the door open, and laying Wesley's body along the back seat.

I ran back in for the rest of them, looking in every room. What the hell is happening? Why can't I get anything to work? Why is my family missing? I look in every room.

Peyton's room—empty.

Mine and Jackie's room—empty.

Where the hell are they? I walk back to the front door, and there's Jackie and Peyton. Both looking me up and down, most likely because I was sweating profusely ever since I entered the house, and my clothes were soaked.

"What are you doing? We've been out in the car for 15 minutes," Jackie snapped, keeping eye contact with me to see if there was something wrong. "Are you okay?"

"I'm fine! Get in the car!" I pushed past them.

I checked my family into the Harmony Palm Master Inn, one of the best hotels I could find, thinking if they were gonna stay in one, they might as well stay in a comfortable one. Peyton harped on me the whole way there, and the whole time checking in. Her and Wesley always got what they wanted—because me and Jackie wanted to give them everything we didn't have growing up. It always makes me feel guilty when I don't abide to this, reminding me that I'm not always gonna be there for them. I didn't want them dealing with anything they didn't have to, the situation with the house being one of them.

In a desperate attempt to make her stop, I said, "I'll be right back! I just want to see what's wrong with the house!" yielding my responses to my daughter as I fled the room.

Back at the house, I stood under the attic door, grabbing the thick rope, pulling the door down, and dropping the stairs in front of me. I made my way up the stairs with a sharp static in my stomach, reaffirming the thought in my head that I've had enough of this. Into the attic, there are two burlap couches, one on the far left side of the room, and the other on the far right. A circular window is on the top part of the wall directly in front of me and the couches. The rest of the room is bare. The couch on the far left had two strips of duct tape on the right cushion, applied in an X formation. The one on the right had a note taped to the cushion. I ripped the note off, reading:

*"My life lies underneath. I'll forever love this house.
Sincerely, Mrs. Holland. September 10, 1899."*

I was fixated on the note with furrowed brows. Bending down to examine underneath the couch, then pushing it aside—I met with the old wooden slabs making the floor. Turning back around to the left couch with the tape in an X on the cushion, glancing back at the right couch, and ripping out the cushions, I'm met with a pile of black and white photos and dozens of wrinkled notes. I stand in place for a second, my head spinning, making me feel off balance, I shake my head and pick up the first photo.

It shows a girl that had to be no older than thirteen, with short, brown hair reaching the back of her neck, and wearing a raggy dress-like cloth—looking to be either black or brown. I turned the photo over to a name on the back,

"Joephine Holland - May 5th 1925"

Who the hell is this woman? Whoever she was, she looked familiar... really familiar. I picked up other photos of her in the same place, but just in different positions. I picked up a note that read:

" I've been given permission to sell this house, but was told

It won't be sold until centuries later."

I thought back to when I was calling about the house, the name the owner gave me, Eugene P. Holland. I reach into my pants pocket for my phone and scrolling through it for the number.

The phone rang.

"Hello?" answered a man with a deadpan northern Atlantic accent.

"Hello? This is Terrance Yates. I was the one who called you about the house before moving in."

A dead silence cut through the air, the same silence before a tornado hits. I felt something was wrong. This didn't feel like a normal conversation. My stomach dropped, making my heart hurt as I cleared my throat.

"So, I just wanted to reconfirm with you about something," I said, taking the phone from my ear, staring at the name Eugene P. Holland on the caller ID. "And that is, are you Eugene P. Holland?"

I'm met with another silence, this one worse than the last.

"Hello?"

The caller ID was still on the phone, along with the call time reading: 15 minutes and 35 seconds. So the line didn't cut, but I couldn't brush off the feeling that I did something wrong, and was confused as to why the room was getting darker.

I put the phone back to my ear. "Hello? Hello?" I asked, begging for reassurance and comfort. "Is Eugene P. Holland, the one that sold me this house?" I demanded, in a stern, wavering voice.

It sounded like the man on the other side picked up the phone. "Yes," he said in a deep deadpan voice.

"Can we meet for lunch sometime?"

It wasn't long until he inserted, void of emotion, "I'm here... I'm here... I'm here..." The voice got raspier every time he said it.

I took the phone away from my ear and hung up. I spotted another black-and-white photo of Joephine Holland standing outside in front of the house. A wooden plaque above the front door read, "Eugene."

Eugene? Why is this—?

I dug through the photos, finding another photo of Joephine and Edna Holland, her mother, standing outside in the front yard, a banner reading in red paint, "Happy birthday Eugene! Glad you're our home!"

As I was digging through the dozens of other photos and notes, I found a note saying that Edna Holland was the fifth resident in the house, four other residents having disappeared before her, along with a note stating Edna's thoughts– saying that she was happy to never find love, and that she was never getting married. Other notes expressed fears of losing her adopted daughter Joephine Holland. But one of the notes stood out to me, saying that Edna named the house after the first year living there. Eugene P. Holland.

I blinked more rapidly and aggressively. My eyes were hurting, my stomach was hurting, and my breathing became more shallow. My head was spinning with thoughts of "I'm never getting out of here" and "Who the fuck was I on the phone with when I bought this house?"

I was skeptical to keep reading. I drug my family into this. What's gonna happen to them? I felt sad for a split second, but then felt... nothing.

I kept reading. On one of the notes I pulled out, it read on the back that she promised she would do anything for it so it wouldn't hurt her or her daughter, knowing the house was special. Another note said that she found a closet in the attic with four picture frames of prior residents on the wall, as well as tapes of the residents' last moments alive.

Still holding the note, I scanned the room, spotting a wooden door behind the couch I was picking notes from, thereby sliding the couch from the door, and opening it. The walls were boarded with picture frames containing prior residents before me. The nothingness I was feeling before got worse. I went blind.

"HEEEELLLP!" I screamed.

Thunk!

Welcome Home Yates: Chapter 2

I took Terrance. I knew it was only a matter of time until Jackie and the kids were coming back to me. Meanwhile, Jackie paced back and forth in the hotel room with the phone to her ear. She called. It went to voicemail. She called again. It went to voicemail. To my delight, she was crying in panic—almost to the point of hysteria—all for the husband that's now part of me.

"This isn't right. He would've called by now," cried Jackie.

Like all humans, she had a horrible intuition that something was wrong. Completely unaware that he was no longer there to protect them, and a mother can only do so much until she's an emotional mess. She called again and was met with a deadline, sending her nerves into a frenzy, tapping on Terrance's name again. Nothing. Deadline. She grabbed her purse. attempting to control her emotions around her kids, feeling like she's moving in slow motion from the looming danger her husband's probably in. No worries, Jackie. I'm waiting for you. Remember? I'm your dream.

Uneasy, Peyton slid off the bed, putting her shoes on,

"I'm coming with you," she insisted, trying to control her fear, which is a beauty to see.

"No, you're not. You're staying here."

Peyton ignored Jackie, and stepped closer.

"Wesley got to go on the last trip with you guys; now I'm coming on this one!"

It pleased me to see her so eager to visit. Jackie sharply exhaled. "Come on," she said, hoping Payton will change her mind.

As they left the room, Wesley darted out of bed, slipped on his shoes, and followed behind.

They thundered into the house, hollering for their father. I watched as the mom searched the garage, and the kids searched the attic. The kids separated from her. I decided to do my part and begin the transformation, making her feel dizzy with no sense of direction, taking away the face that the kids called "mom"— by swelling up her eyes and starving her. Not long after, I decided to make her lock the garage door before making her body shake in pain. Screaming in pain on the garage floor as we hear in the house—

"Mom?— Mom!" cried Peyton, her voice spiked with panic. Beautiful. Just beautiful.

The kids tugged on the garage door, jerking the door harder and harder as I have the mom scream in pain. Where's Terrance? Where's Mommy? The screaming descended into moaning, then that moaning into loud screeching. Complimenting it with heartfelt crying for her kids. Peyton cried as Wesley stood in terror, crying behind her. Now it's time for the grand finale! I made the whole house go completely silent. The mom– gone. Peyton and Wesely froze with tears running down their cheeks.

"Mom?" Peyton says, shaking, forehead furrowed in confusion.

The house is filled with a deafening silence, noise only coming from outside, but the outside noise sounds like it's miles away. Peyton and Wesley stand in place, glancing around, listening to their ears ring and heads buzz as the silence gets denser. Peyton twisted the knob, keeping it in place before whispering, "1. 2. 3." She yanked the door open to an empty garage, striding over to each side,

"Mom? Mom? Please answer me!"

After she checked each side of the room, knocked over boxes, opened the door leading to the backyard, then wandered back to the knocked-over boxes, where she stood in place for a minute; back facing Wesley before,

"I WANT MY CAR! WHERE'S MY FUCKING CAR?" screamed Peyton in a screeching voice, crying into her hands before throwing a box at the garage door.

Both stood there, Wesley staring at her, trying to figure out what to say to make her feel better. Peyton sat crisscrossed in the middle of the garage with her arms limp in her lap. Wesley plodded cautiously towards her, sitting beside her. A clock ticked as an unintentional reminder that the danger's still moving, punctuating the wasting opportunity to save themselves. This is most likely because they're used to pushing urgent and challenging matters on their parents, letting them deal with the heavy weight, while they sit around waiting for it to be fixed. I thought this was it. I thought they were sitting targets for me to take, but to my indignation, Wesley gasped, and rushed to the attic. Peyton glanced up with tears on her cheeks, then followed.

Wesley made his way up the attic stairs.

"What are you doing?" inquired Peyton, kindled with concealed excitement, yet confused.

Wesley dug through the notes and photos inside the couch. "Where is it? Where is it?" His eyes light up, "Ha," he said, pulling out a picture of Joephine and Edna standing in front of the house with a birthday banner and balloons.

"What? What's that?" Peyton, bewildered and eager.

"It's a photo I found while digging through the attic one night." Wesley gazes at it with intrigue.

"Are you serious? Mom told you not to come up here!" Peyton thundered. Her nose and eyes have slightly swollen since entering the attic.

Wesley noticed but didn't say anything. Standing up and flipping the photo over, he read:

"Dear Eugene. I promise you won't be replaced, for I know you were stuffed with drywall and destroyed last time, and I'll do anything in my power to not let it happen again. Sincerely, My Sweet Sentient House, Mrs. Holland."

He glanced up at Peyton, both sharing a gaze, though clearly not thinking the same thing.

Peyton's nose and eyes were swelling. "So? Those are like from the fifties. Wesley. They don't mean anything."

Wesley walked into the attic closet, coming out with a new picture frame with a photo of their dad inside. She grabbed the picture, fraught with mixed emotions.

"I found that while digging around up here," Wesley inserts. "And it says on one of the notes that the last house was alive. Dean Starks, the last owner of the first house, stuffed it with drywall and destroyed it before dying in the 1900's. It's said that the house still had a hold on him."

Peyton gazed at the picture, then strode over to the couch and picked up notes confirming what Wesley said. Her nose and eyes were getting worse. "Okay, so what do we do?" she asked.

Wesley reached out. "Can I see your phone?"

She handed it to him, and he called their grandparents to pick them up, explaining that mom and dad were gone.

About thirty minutes later, my sister and I were picked up by our grandparents, who helped us talk to the police about how our mom and dad had disappeared. Showing them the bizarre photo of my dad that was distorted and faded.

Peyton and I begged them to stuff the house with drywall and tear it down, telling them the disturbing history of the line of residents that have disappeared here.

Two months after talking to the police, my sister and I got the news that the house was stuffed and destroyed.

I'm Cody Matthews! I didn't always start with writing books, in fact, my dream was to become a script writer for mature cartoons on tv: like the simpsons and south park. A lot of my stories for these scripts I practiced writing were full of dark humor, whether if that was a younger sister killing people and stealing her mom's credit cards to go to a theme park; or if that was a mom character losing her mind, then starting a crappy comedy special on netflix. This is the stuff I wrote. It wasn't until later that my biological mom suggested writing books or short stories, something I didn't seriously consider, just because I was DEAD set on writing tv scripts. Granted, I had short stories in mind that I wanted to write. One of them was a magician that psychologically torments two siblings after they discover and open a dead magician's magic kit. Magicians still freak me out! Glad I'm not these kids! Anyways. Skip ahead. Several months ago, while prolifically posting on a FB horror story group, just seeing what kind of criticism I could get from my stories. I was messaged by Jake. And the next thing I knew, I was buying a book on amazon containing dozens of short stories by talented aspiring authors, including myself.

WHISPER KINDLY
AS WE CROSS

K.L. Rasmussen

Secrets never stay buried. No matter how deep you bury them, they will resurface at some point. Whether by accident or someone digs them up by happenchance. As I took those first steps towards Danny's El Camino, I knew I should have stayed home tonight. I could have stayed out of trouble rather than followed the crowd. Read a book or binge-watch 90 Day Fiance with Mom. Either plan would've been better than what we encountered.

Cecelia, girls your age should be out having fun.

Yeah, fun. And that's all coming to a crashing end here as graduation approaches in just a few short weeks. Which why I forced myself to go out, because soon I will be thrust into the perils of adulthood. These are supposed to be my best years of making memories. Rest assured—I will remember this night too well.

It began the minute I opened the rumbling car door, and sat in the back seat with Sophie and Kyle, who couldn't keep their hands to themselves. Going to separate colleges is going to be hell for them. They've been macking on each other since day one.

Danny grinned at me from the front seat, feeling victorious that he'd finally dragged me out of my witch cave.

"You can't hide away from us forever, Cece," he says as he pulls the car out from the driveway. "Yeah! Get your nose out of those books and let loose. You'll have plenty of time in college to lose your mind in a book," Anna says from the front seat, stroking Danny's knee with her manicured claws. She's had her hooks in him since freshman year, leaving me to be the fifth wheel. Pining in the back seat, wishing that it was me in her place.

It should have been, but I can't hold onto that forever. High school is ending. I convinced myself that this was a good idea. That is, until Danny reveals the plan.

"So my Uncle Ronnie was donated a whole bunch of state-of-the-art fireworks. I stuffed what I could sneak from his truck into the trunk. I thought we'd go out to the old woods and celebrate. Enter this world with a bang!" Danny bounces in the driver's seat with childlike excitement. Something I always admired about him - his ability to go from zero to one hundred in a matter of seconds. His ability to find the joy and excitement in the simplest of things. I don't know if I've ever experienced this joy. Or have the ability to. If it ever existed. Since grade school my life has been all real-world situations, I didn't allow much room for fantasy, except for the books that allowed me to escape there.

Anna rolls her eyes but kisses him on the cheek forcefully, Danny is too hyped to notice, turning up the radio blasting Metallica. I wonder how their love story will play out after high school. Danny has a future working in his uncle's garage, while Anna has been accepted on scholarship to UCLA. Danny is wild and chaotic, while Anna has always been the uptight, to-do-list kind of girl. She keeps Danny organized.

Kyle and Sophie are whispering, staring deep into each other's eyes. They were in their little world and I had no desire to intrude. Being the fifth wheel. That's what I signed up for for tonight. I hope that in college I can either continue my future as a never-been-kissed spinster or at least there is some hope for me.

With no protests to the plan, we zoom down the rolling hills and watch the nightlife crawl to the streets. The El Camino fires down the main strip of the town lit by the phantasmal glow of ornate lights. Lined with neon star signs and motels for tourists, College students travel in bulk groups migrating their way to the bars, and the scattered homeless chase down their charity prospects and dart traffic. Ghostlike figures conceal themselves down the dark alleys, always evading the land of the living but throwing hints of their existence.

Do they want to be seen or not? Or do they plan to hide away forever?

I loved watching the outside world pass us by, I got so lost looking out the window that I barely noticed Danny calling out to me "Earth to Cece!"

My ability to disassociate was unsettling at times.

"We're stopping for drinks at the QT. Want anything? My treat." He smiles like he means it, and like it's a partial apology for leaving me alone with the girls. I've always gotten along better with the boys.

"Just a coke, please," I ask sheepishly. It felt weird having Danny buy something for me. Sure, it's just a coke, and Danny's been my friend since before he and Anna even saw each other that way. But some part of me felt like I was intruding on what they had.

It's hard to believe that Danny and Anna have been together as long as they have, let alone at all. They hated each other, they were always at each other's throats. It was lost on me the day that they first kissed in the halls, shocking the world around them. It's like it happened overnight. Not in a million years would anyone have put them together. They're so different from each other. And the snapshots of them play on repeat in my head. I had to swallow the pill and move on - focus on the future outside of high school, crushes, and girl gossip.

I already felt like an outsider here, the girls didn't need to say it. I've not been around to participate in the girl talks and the drama. I've been at home - with my nose in a book, waiting for someone to call and whisk me away. Maybe they've been waiting for a call from me. The phone works both ways.

The car lurches to a halt as Danny parks in front of the QuikTrip and runs in with Kyle to collect the goodies, leaving us ladies alone to chat - and immediately, I was lost to what the conversation was about. Our friends Jeremy and Stephanie had a falling out and are demanding their friends to take sides. What the actual argument was about was the topic of conversation. As they say, there are so many sides to one story.

"What do you think, Cece?" Anna turns to me, and a smirk plays across her face. I freeze, I didn't even expect them to care what I think, I've been out of the loop. It's her showing how obvious it is. What do I even talk about with these people?

"I honestly don't know enough to have an opinion, I'm sorry."

"How diplomatic of you. That will surely work when you get to Harvard or wherever the fuck you're going." Anna goes back to filing her nails and flipping throw Danny's phone to choose a new song only to settle on Midnights by the one and only Taylor Swift. Anna checks her tour dates religiously, just waiting to find Taylor Swift in our small town. We'd have to drive to the valley after selling our souls to Ticketmaster. I've heard some people paid well over a month's rent to go to her concert. And Anna wasn't beyond that. To her that was her weekly pocket money. I just live vicariously through other people's videos they post online. Thank god for them.

Sophie gives me a sympathetic look and mouths 'sorry' so that Anna can't see in the reflection of her phone screen. I shrug. I am not going to let it affect the night, but already I can see how this night is going to end. Or so I thought.

The boys hop back in the car with a bag of snacks, ignoring the change of energy that bounced against the windows. Or at least Kyle did. You'd think that he and Sophie were separated for a lifetime with the way he kissed her so passionately. They are soaking up every moment they have left with each other. While Danny wrestles Anna for control of the music. "But it's her new release of the song, I just want to hear it one more time," Anna argues, using the soft voice she reserves emotional manipulation. Softening her eyes and batting lashes, as if she were about to cry in mere seconds of hearing the word no. A word I don't know if she's heard definitively in her life.

Soon we were driving tall dominating pine trees, and yellow glowing eyes peeking through the underbrush, scoping out if the coast is clear, only to tear away into the darkness again at the first flash of a headlight. I've only seen a few elk hidden in these trees. For the most part, only the scattering unkindness of ravens can be found flocking through these woods. Daniel ignores Anna as she continues to argue for her 'turn' on the music, I smile to myself. It was a small petty victory but I will take it as I sip the coke her boyfriend bought me.

The crunch of the gravel path Daniel turns down is unsettling. We were the farthest we could be from town, with very little around us except the wilderness. Pulling off to a designated camper park, Daniel shuts the engine off and is out of the car unloading the trunk of fireworks before any of us can unbuckle our belts and gather our bearings. I offer to take a bag of snacks and my coke. I stick my phone in my back pocket, leaving my purse behind. It's not like I am going to need it out here. We're just going to shoot off some fireworks and talk about old times and enjoy not being in town. For me, this was a nice change from the normal backsplash of the wall my desk sits against and the classroom. Or the library. It was nice switching it up. Daniel is carrying two duffle bags that I assumed were stuffed to the brim with fireworks, wearing a boyish grin. Danny loves playing with fire. Always has and always will.

He leads us down a narrow path that disappears into a thicket of trees, spinny branches reach threatening, snagging our clothes as we brush past.

"Where are you leading us to, Dannyboy?" Kyle asks, peeking behind us as we push further away from the car. The only sound that could be heard was the snapping of twigs under our feet.

This reminded me of the days we'd sneak out and hike the canyons and more elusive hiking trails. Incredibly dangerous and now looking back, I wonder how we made it home alive. "You ever hear of the story about Raven's Bridge?" Danny calls from the front. "Oh come on, you don't believe in ghost stories, Danny," Kyle says from the rear, we girls fill the gap with nervous giggles.

"No, no hear me out. Raven's Bridge, it's real. The stories. Do you remember Matt Lornhoven? He said he was poking around here at night, hoping to catch a game of rabbits with a slingshot and a bowing knife - fucking idiot, anyways not the point. He swears as he was crossing the bridge he saw, just waiting for him at the other side some kind of fucked up raven-man-thing," Danny goes on. "He told me he had heard this strange croaking voice echo in his head as if the voice was whispering directly in his ear. Exposing all of his darkest thoughts, exploiting his deepest fantasies. I think it eventually drove him mad."

"Didn't that kid end up as a quadriplegic after a boating accident with his cousin?" Kyle retorts. "It was the madness that drove him to it," Danny says ominously.

"He was drunk and didn't have his license."

"He was drunk...with madness."

"What eighteen-year-old has secrets that drive them into madness?" Kyle says so innocently. What eighteen-year-old doesn't have secrets?

There were some in my class who had spent the night in jail as opposed to calling home to be bailed out. How they hid the aftermath is beyond me. There are some stories that I am waiting until I am in my thirties and no longer living under my mother's roof before I confess to her some of the stupid shit has happened. Like that time her minivan was stolen and used in a drive-by shooting. Mom was on a work trip and left the house with the keys and the van.

I had a party, got too drunk, and passed out. I didn't find out that the car was taken until I found the gun shells in the backseat.

There was a lot that was unclear about that night.

"It's true. I visited him in hospice. He told me everything. He said that the Unkindness drove him to it."

Anna and Sophie shudder. I let out a nervous laugh. It's just a ghost story Danny is using to spook us. Always looking for a good laugh. Anything to cause excitement. He's like that, one of the many things that I admire about him.

"Well if anything happens, I got my knife on me," Kyle says, to reassure Sophie. Yeah, sure a knife. But it's not a gun.

I leave it alone and continue to follow, he said that for Sophie and Anna, who I am sure haven't wielded a weapon of any sort in their lifetime, but feel safe having a man around who is armed and ready to play knight in shining armor against any threat.

Danny jokes a lot, but that doesn't stop the chills from setting in on the back of my neck and a hollowness building in my stomach.

What happened to Matt Lornhoven was terrible. I still remember the photos from the hospital, his body nearly mangled by the boat propellor. He's still in intensive care. Danny was so worried when he got the call about the accident, I've never seen him so distraught.

We reach a small grassy clearing that still smelled of the burnt remnants of a bonfire - a smoldering glow still held in the rubble. I stomp it out, marking the time in my head with a glance at my phone. I imagine the fire's brilliance and glow. To spend an evening with friends around a well-built fire, part of me feels envious to have not been a part of it. Despite it being a no-burning zone. It's too dry, and wildfires are quickly wiping out the west coast. Part of me fears that setting fireworks off isn't wise.

A few items had been left behind in the rubble and ash. A set of keys and what looked like an ID. I pick it up and find that it belongs to Mr. Rigby, our math teacher who had gone on sabbatical recently. It seemed odd he would leave in the middle of the term just like that. He was always so dedicated, pristine, and put together - his appearance became more disheveled and unkempt. Beard was overgrown and scruffily, drooping eyes, and always had a dry cough. He could be heard hacking up a lung three classrooms away. Something was eating away at this man - could it be what drove Matt insane? Why was Mr. Rigby out here? Was he still lurking about? Danny looked at me - he knew I knew he wasn't kidding around when he told that story. For once he was serious.

Why did Danny bring us here tonight?

I pocketed the keys and the ID. He lives just down the block from my house, I can just leave them in his mailbox. Danny led us to the continuing path of trees that travel downward, closer to the water.

The branches and thorns tugged at my arms as I pushed through, following Danny much closer than before. Anna and Sophie trailed behind clutching to Kyle.

We reach the shoreline of the glistening creek with a stone arch bridge, cast in the moonlight breaking through the trees above. The other side was dark and unlit. Who knew what lurked on the other side? The boys waste no time, unpacking the fireworks and organizing them according to type. Danny had a whole show planned for us. I can't relax. I am nervous - there are too many coincidences here. I cross my arms, barring myself from the cold. Sophie and

Anna stick close together, near the edge of the bridge. They begin to relax and dig into their snacks. Part of me wishes we had brought lawn chairs or something. I step towards the stone arch bridge, ignoring the gasps behind me. I hop up on the ledge cross my legs and attempt to find comfort sitting on this ominous bridge.

Had Danny not said anything, would I still have this feeling that we are being watched? I glance around me but all I see is the low glow of the blue moonlight bouncing off the dark wood surrounding us. The canal flows under us with a soft trickle that almost sounds like the fluttering of fairy wings dancing in the air and spreading their magic.

"So, Cecelia, you're going to Harvard, right?" Kyle begins, cracking open a Monster. "Yep, Psychology."

"And what do you want to do with that?"

"I want to be a forensic psychologist."

"So, like FBI?"

"Exactly."

"Aw shit, you're going to be a badass," Kyle laughs.

I could hear the steam teeming off Anna. She hated that I was getting any sort of attention from anyone. I never understood her need to compete with me.

She's going to UCLA. I don't know what she's doing, and I'm not giving her the satisfaction of asking.

She then turned her attention to the one thing she knew she could dangle in my face - Danny, who was still too focused on lining up the fireworks in a certain order to make the perfect show, hardly paying any mind to the performance of affection Anna was giving. Leaning up on him and trying to cuddle, he pushed her off of him, "Anna, I'm busy right now."

Anna crossed her arms and huffed dramatically before joining Sophie and me on the wall. Sophie had decided if I was okay to sit up there, so was she. Nothing had grabbed me and pulled me under the bridge. Yet.

The prickle of a thousand eyes on us still crept down the hairs of my neck.

Anna didn't speak, and yet again lost herself in her phone, taking selfies and replying to a Snapchat. I was surprised she still got service out here. I wasn't that lucky. "So when does term start for you?" I make awkward small talk with Sophie and Kyle. We get lost in talking about the different clubs we want to join, and dreams of studying abroad in the UK or Africa.

Anna huffed, still refusing to give her input willingly. She wants to be asked. But we ran out of time.

"Alright folks, it's time for the show we've all been waiting for," Danny announces, lining the first few on the opposite side of the bridge.

Pulling out a lighter he sets the first of many on the bridge, a simple rocket-shaped one, and sets the wick alight and quickly steps back. Sophie and I jump off the ledge and back off from the bridge.

Anna stays put - to show she's not afraid. She's always trying to show off, why she's the best. I've never understood that about her, and it put a wedge between us.

The firework soars into the night sky from the edge of the bridge painting the darkness with bursts of color, illuminating the canal below with shimmering light like fairy dust scattering about. It felt truly enchanting - for a moment it felt as if no time had passed. My eyes met Danny's and we both lingered there, sharing in a conversation that only we understood. I miss you.

Danny's eyes flicker away and escapes to light the next firework, which explodes in flames of red, much like Anna's face. Burning red with envy. Cigarettes After Sex begins to play on portable Bluetooth speakers and Anna takes this moment to throw her arms around Danny, forcing him to slow dance as the rocket he'd lit launches off above them. Danny humors her and spins her a few times, but appears annoyed. That was dangerous.

He sets her down to her feet and scowls at her as he walks away. He places the next firework down towards the center of the stone bridge and sets a large cylindrical firework on the ground. This girl couldn't take the hint that Danny just wasn't that guy. He didn't want to be used in her make-believe mindfucking games. He's outgrown her already, and it's showing. And she finally sees it now being altogether - this was what she dreaded. The truth is that we were always meant to part ways. It's never easy, and sometimes people will do anything to make the parting hard - so they stay or cut off entirely. Rip the relationship up like a bandaid. The sting will eventually fade away.

The large cylindrical firework sprouted like a fountain, spilling beads of colorful light from its sparky spout. Two more after that shot into the sky, weaving around each other like ribbons and then exploding simultaneously sending colorful sparks in every direction. Sophie and Kyle cheer and kiss. Anna is distraught, feeling the despair of her boyfriend pushing her away. Daniel is preparing for the grand finale, excited and living in the moment. And I am here - watching from the sidelines. Like a fly on the wall, here to see how this chapter ends. "Everyone ready!"

We all cheer, except Anna.

Everything is about to come undone, a foreign voice hums in my ear.

"Let 'em rip, Dannyboy!" Kyle shouts.

Danny flicks the lighter and sets four big rockets off at once. They scream into the air like flying comets and burst and crackle. We cheer it on to continue, sulking in the excitement, knowing it will be short-lived. After this. Everything changes.

Our cheers die as the crackles dissipate into an eerie silence. Smoke hangs on the bridge, and the scent of a burnt match lingers.

Across the bridge, two large yellow eyes can be seen.

No one moves. No one speaks.

Except for the Unkindness in our hearts.

Every bitter feeling I've kept silent these past few months comes rising to the surface. The night before Danny and Anna became a couple, Danny was at my house. Had kissed me, and expressed feelings of going steady. When school came the next day, it was like he'd forgotten me. My heart shattered into a billion pieces when I saw him kiss Anna. And she smiled. She won.

What had happened the moment after he had dropped me at the front door and kissed me with such tenacity and passion? The feeling of his kiss, the bite on my lip has stung where he left them. I know why I stopped hanging out with these guys - they're assholes.

From the darkness of the smoke approaches a monstrous raven, with eyes that glowed so brightly yellow. No one spoke or moved. Not even to scream or run in fear. You can never evade what haunts your heart.

Danny. He hurt me, yet I still miss him. Anna, she hates me. Kyle and Sophie are screaming at each other about who would give up first - Anna is begging Danny to just even show her a

moment of passion and romance - but his eyes are locked on me. And I couldn't look away from the path that led the fuck out of here.

"We're done, Anna. I told you this three times- yet you want to continue to act like a couple. You invited yourself out here and are mad I am not giving you the attention that you want. Have fun at UCLA fucking up some other dude."

Danny puts some distance between him and Anna. Tears strike Anna's face. The humiliation, the rejection.

"So that's it - I can't even be close to you as a friend? Like we can't hug?" Anna sobs, reaching out for him.

Damn. Sophie and Kyle stopped their argument to tune into Danny and Anna's. "Anna, I don't mean it like that. But it seems as if you don't get that we've broken up. It doesn't seem like anything has changed. It wasn't a good idea for you to come out here." It's not good for any of you to be out here in my woods, the voice croaked again. More yellow eyes glint in the darkness of the trees.

"Guys, we can continue this later, but we should probably leave," I suggest, my voice quivering in fear. A cacophony of whispers fills my mind, each word dripping with malice and deceit. I couldn't drown it out.

"Oh sure, now you pipe up! Just when you get to watch my life fall apart." "Um, no, but I am prett-"

"Shut the fuck up. You just have to be right all the time, don't you, Cecelia?" Anna advances on me, her knuckles balled up. I back away, ready to run up the path back to the car. This girl is about ready to fight me. Over what? A guy who probably doesn't give a shit about either one of us. Her ego.

"Anna, stop it!" Danny bellows ready to take after me.

You will all reap what you sow, the Unkindness speaks. We all stop in our tracks as the large monstrous creature spreads its wings and vanishes into the shadows, leaving behind only the haunting silence that echoed through these ominous woods. A fog settled around us - I couldn't see a thing around me except the opening to the path we took to get here. A shadow with red piercing eyes recoils into the shadows, enticing me to follow with the beckoning of a long scraggly finger that resembled a talon. I tear after it.

The sound of twigs crunching and branches snapping under my feet crack in my eardrums as I tear down the path, desperate to get to a road or somewhere I can get a ride. I couldn't bear to spend another hour with these people. We weren't friends - we were strangers playing a part. This was another game. Another scene in the Danny & Anna Show.

I heard footsteps, the sounds of heavy breathing. For a second - my name. The sound of fluttering wings and the caw of a dark bird chase me further down the path. The opening to the clearing lies just a few paces ahead - I push forward, feeling the strain and exhaustion on my legs want to give out from underneath me. But I can't - I'm almost there.

Crash-landing in the grass in the clearing by the fire pit, I catch my breath for a moment. The sky above spins in circles and spirals. I close my eyes and listen for the sound of the others escaping, landing beside me and taking a joint breath of relief that we made it out alive. But it never came.

It was only me.

I search through the trees for any sign of movement. The branches were still and no laughter or screaming fell through the trees.

I start screaming names. Danny's. Anna's. Kyle's.

I bring my hands up to my face to call louder - I shudder as soon as something thick and wet touches my face.

Blood.

What have I done?

K.L Rasmussen is a passionate writer immersed in Victorian and Gothic literature. By day, she shares her love for books as a knowledgeable bookseller at Barnes & Noble. With her feline companion, Minerva, as my muse, she brings stories to life with captivating words and detailed illustrations.

Want More From The

Sinister Society?

Follow along on our social medias
@sinistersociety

&

Join our Facebook Group for submissions
calls and latest updates!
https://www.facebook.com/groups/1444531013102495

www.ingramcontent.com/pod-product-compliance
Lightning Source LLC
Chambersburg PA
CBHW061549310726
48972CB00008B/2674